THE BOBBSEY TWINS
AND THE GOLDFISH MYSTERY

THE BOBBSEY TWINS
By Laura Lee Hope

"Oh, look!" Flossie exclaimed as the first kite
came into view

The Bobbsey Twins
and the
Goldfish Mystery

By

LAURA LEE HOPE

GROSSET & DUNLAP
Publishers   *New York*

ISBN: 0-448-08055-9
© GROSSET & DUNLAP, INC., 1962
ALL RIGHTS RESERVED

The Bobbsey Twins and the Goldfish Mystery

CONTENTS

THE BOBBSEY TWINS
AND THE GOLDFISH MYSTERY

CHAPTER I

A GOLDFISH RESCUE

"OOH, Freddie!" cried six-year-old Flossie Bobbsey. "See that funny fish in the corner! Its eyes are popping out of its head!"

Flossie and her blond, blue-eyed twin pressed their noses against a large glass fish tank. It stood on a table in the entrance hall of the Lakeport Aquarium.

"It looks like a pollywog." Freddie giggled as he watched the tropical fish swim in and out among the plants in the tank bottom. Some fish were almost round with skinny, flat bodies. Others had long noses and short tails.

At that moment Flossie gave a little scream. "Oh! Something's running down my back!"

Freddie whirled just in time to see an older boy replace the filter hose in the fish tank.

"Danny Rugg!" Freddie cried out. "You squirted water on Flossie!"

1

Danny, a stocky boy of twelve, was a bully and often played mean tricks on the Bobbseys and their friends. Now he pretended to be surprised and asked, "What makes you think I did that?"

"You did, and on purpose, too!" Freddie said hotly.

"What's going on here?" a slender, dark-haired boy of Danny's age demanded, as he came toward the three children.

He was Bert Bobbsey, the twins' twelve-year-old brother. "Why don't you pick on someone your own size, Danny?" he said scornfully.

Danny sneered, "You Bobbsey twins never could take a joke!"

At the sound of the boys' angry voices, the aquarium director, who was passing through the hall, stopped. He walked over to them and said, "All right, boys, that's enough arguing. Now, if you children will come into the next room, I'll show you an unusual Japanese goldfish. All goldfish, by the way, came from Japan originally."

"I don't want to see any old goldfish," Danny muttered, and stalked from the building.

Bert, Freddie, and Flossie followed Mr. Walton, the director, into the adjoining room. It was lined with glass tanks set into the wall.

Here and there stood a tank on a pedestal. Fish of all kinds were swimming in the tanks.

A dark-haired girl with sparkling brown eyes stood in front of one display. "Oh, there you are, Nan," Bert called to his twin sister. "Mr. Walton is going to show us a special Japanese goldfish."

Nan ran over to the group. "Did it really come all the way from Japan, Mr. Walton?" she asked.

"Indeed it did," the director replied. "This is a very peculiar variety of fish. In fact," he added with a smile, "these fish can hardly swim."

"A fish that can't swim!" Freddie exclaimed.

Mr. Walton led the way to a tank containing a strange-looking fish. It had a feathery tail and a large, knobby head.

"This one is called an Azumanishiki in Japan," he explained.

"Has-a-man-a-sheeky?" Flossie giggled. "What does that name mean?"

The director laughed. "It would be easier if you said Lion-headed Veiltail. That's what we call it in this country."

"Does it roar like a lion?" Freddie asked excitedly, and the others laughed.

"No, but it's a very rare fish," Mr. Walton replied. "This is the only Veiltail specimen we've ever had in this country. It's worth a great deal of money."

He reached into the water, holding some food in a pair of tweezers. The odd fish swam up clumsily and nibbled the food.

"It really can't swim very well, can it?" Bert commented with a grin.

"No," Mr. Walton replied. "That's why we feed it with tweezers. Poor old Veiltail's movements are so slow that it can't compete with other fish for food. In Japan, the Lion-headed Veiltails are fed with chopsticks!"

"Chopstick tweezers," said Bert, smiling.

After the children had left the aquarium, Nan said, "I'd love to own some goldfish. Let's stop in the variety store and buy a few."

"Oh, yes, let's!" Flossie urged.

"Okay," Bert answered. "We still have that old fish bowl at home."

The twins hurried to the store and went in. At the rear, on a counter, stood a tank filled with goldfish of many varieties.

"Have you any goldfish with lions' heads?" Freddie asked the young saleswoman.

The clerk smiled. "I'm afraid not," she said. "But here's a nice one." She pointed to a fish that was almost white and had bright red fins.

"It's bee-yoo-ti-ful!" Flossie exclaimed. "Let's buy that one!"

The others agreed. The saleswoman put water from the tank into a cardboard container. Then with a little net, she scooped up the red-and-white fish. Next, she flipped it into the container.

She was about to turn away when Freddie cried out, "Oh! Let's get that one, too!"

He pointed to a bright-orange fish which darted through the water. "He's a good swimmer!"

At Bert's nod, the clerk added the orange fish to the one in the carton. Bert paid for the fish and some food for them. Then the twins left the store. Freddie proudly carried the little box.

Flossie skipped along beside her twin. "Won't it be fun having goldfish, Freddie?" she bubbled. "We can have our own 'quarium and invite people to see our fish!"

"Watch the traffic light!" Nan called.

At that moment the signal turned red. Freddie and Flossie obediently stopped at the curb. Suddenly, Danny Rugg came racing up the side street. *Smack!* He bumped into Freddie and ran on.

The force of the collision knocked the carton from the little boy's hands. It fell to the sidewalk, and the two fish flopped out!

The carton fell to the sidewalk, and the two
fish flopped out!

"Oh!" Flossie cried. "The water's spilled! Our fish will die!"

Just before Nan and Bert reached their brother and sister, a black-haired girl about eight years old dashed up. Quickly she scooped the gasping fish into the carton. Each one gave a flop and then lay still.

"Please come with me," the little girl urged. "I will try to save your fish!"

The Bobbseys did not stop to ask questions. They hurried along with the girl to a nearby house. "This is where I live," she said. "I am Jane Naga. Please come in."

Jane led them to the kitchen. The twins introduced themselves as she made preparations for saving the fish. With lightning speed she collected four glass bowls and took them to the sink. One bowl she filled with cold water and another with warm. Into the other two bowls she ran lukewarm water. Then she measured out three tablespoonfuls of salt and poured it into one of the bowls containing lukewarm water.

"Ooh!" Flossie wailed. "Hurry! Our fish look dead already."

Jane put the two limp fish into the cold water, counted to five, then dropped them into the warm water. The fish were still quiet. Then she laid the fish in the salted water, and finally put them into the fourth bowl. As she did this, the red-and-white fish gave a feeble wiggle.

"It's coming to!" Nan cried. The next second, the other fish started to swim feebly.

"They're alive! They're alive!" Freddie shouted, peering into the fourth bowl.

The twins had been so interested watching Jane work with the fish that they had not noticed a little boy standing in the doorway. He had the same wiry black hair and dark eyes as Jane.

"This is my brother Jimmy," Jane explained. "He's seven."

Jimmy smiled shyly, as the twins said hello. "I'm glad your fish are all right," he spoke up.

"So are we," Nan said happily. "Thank you for saving them, Jane. We wouldn't have known what to do!"

"Jimmy and I are Japanese," Jane replied. "There are many goldfish in Japan, and we have been taught how to care for them."

"Japan!" Nan exclaimed. "How exciting! Were you born there?"

Jane shook her head. "No. Our father left and came to California. That's where we were born. Our family moved to Lakeport last month."

Flossie spoke up. "You and Jimmy must come

over to our house and play with us twins."

"We'd like to." Jane smiled.

"May we carry our fish home in your bowl?" Freddie asked the Naga children.

"Oh, yes, of course," Jane answered.

"We'll bring the bowl back tomorrow," Nan promised. The twins said good-by and started off once more.

When they reached their large, comfortable house, the front door was opened by a stout, jolly-looking colored woman. She was Dinah Johnson, who had helped Mrs. Bobbsey with the cooking and housework as long as Bert and Nan could remember. Her husband Sam drove a truck at Mr. Bobbsey's lumberyard. The couple lived in a third-floor-rear apartment of the house.

Dinah looked suspiciously at the glass fish bowl which Freddie was holding. "What you got there?" she asked.

"Japanese goldfish," Flossie said proudly. "We're going to start a 'quarium!"

The jolly cook chuckled. "Well, before you do that, you all better get fixed up for supper. Company's coming," she said mysteriously, and walked back to the kitchen.

The four children went into the dining room where a slim, pretty woman was setting the table. "Who's coming to supper, Mother?" Nan asked her curiously.

Mrs. Bobbsey smiled at the four eager faces. "Your father is bringing home a Japanese gentleman," she replied. "He is in the lumber business in Japan. They'll be here shortly."

The children hurried up to their rooms to put on fresh clothes. "Isn't it funny, Nan?" Flossie remarked. "We've heard Japan three times to-day—the goldfish, Jane, and Jimmy, and now Daddy's friend!"

"I wonder what he'll be like?" Nan mused.

When the children entered the living room a little later, they found that their tall, good-looking father and his guest had arrived. The twins were introduced to the visitor, a slender man of medium height. He wore thick-lensed glasses over his brown eyes.

"This is Mr. Mino Naga from Kyoto, Japan," Mr. Bobbsey said. "He is spending a few days in Lakeport."

"Naga!" Bert exclaimed. "Oh, how do you do, sir?"

All the children shook hands, then Freddie asked, "Do you know Jane and Jimmy Naga?"

Their visitor looked surprised. "Why, I am staying at their home! They are my niece and nephew. You have met them?"

"Oh, yes," Flossie cried. "Jane saved our gold-fish when Danny made Freddie spill them out of the box and we thought they were dead!" She stopped, a little breathless.

Just then Dinah came to the door and announced that dinner was served. The Bobbseys and their guest went to the table.

"I was very glad to see my brother and his family. We Japanese have a strong family feeling," Mr. Naga continued, after grace had been said. He looked sad for a moment. "I had two other brothers, but they are gone."

"It's nice, though, that you are able to visit at your brother's home while you're in Lakeport," Mrs. Bobbsey said.

Mr. Naga nodded. "I am only sorry that I cannot remain with them longer. But I must return to Japan immediately."

Mr. Bobbsey looked very surprised. "Really? I understood you were to be in our country for some time!"

"Such was indeed my plan," Mr. Naga replied. "But I learned today from my wife that a very valuable family possession has disappeared!"

CHAPTER II

TWO MYSTERIES

"DISAPPEARED!" Bert echoed. "Something valuable's gone, Mr. Naga?"

"A very precious gold bracelet belonging to my wife is missing. She had lent it to the museum in Kyoto, where we live. I am afraid the bracelet has been stolen. I will tell you about it."

Mr. Naga explained that his oldest brother, Akio, who had died recently, had been a famous artist in Japan.

"Akio was best known for his paintings, but he also made beautiful things from metal. His last accomplishment was the gold bracelet, which he left to my wife. And now it is gone!"

"I'm sure it will be found," Nan said kindly.

Mr. Naga smiled at her. "I hope so. In the cable from my wife informing me of the loss, she said that the Kyoto police are already working on the case. But I wish to return home and see if I can help."

After dessert, everyone went into the living room. Flossie waited until everyone else was seated, then she walked over to the chair which Mr. Naga had taken.

"I wish you didn't have to go away so soon," she said to him.

"I also wish the same." The Japanese smiled at the little girl, then turned to Mr. Bobbsey and said, "If you will cable me when you leave, Richard, I will meet you in Tokyo."

"Tokyo!"

"Are you going to Japan, Daddy?"

"When?"

"Please tell us about it!"

The twins plied their father with excited questions. Laughingly he put up his hands. "Just a minute," he begged. "I'll explain."

When the twins became quiet, Mr. Bobbsey went on. "A friend of mine in New York is starting a business to manufacture toys and small carved decorations made of wood. He suggested that I consult Mr. Naga, and then, since I'm in the lumber business, investigate the wood in Japan. If I think it's suitable, I'm to buy some for him."

"We have very fine trees in my country," Mr.

Naga told the twins. "I am going to show your father the Japanese cedar, which we call cryptomeria. It is especially good for making toys and wood carvings."

"Oh boy! The trip sounds great, Dad!" Bert exclaimed. "You'll be able to tell us all about Japan!"

"Daddy," Flossie spoke up, "will you bring me back a has-a-man-a-sheeky?"

Mr. Bobbsey looked puzzled. "I'd be glad to, my little fat fairy, but what is it?" This was Mr. Bobbsey's nickname for his younger daughter. He called Freddie his little fat fireman because he liked to play with his toy fire engine and wanted to be a fireman when he grew up.

Flossie giggled. *"You* know what I mean, don't you?" she asked Mr. Naga.

The visitor chuckled, and said, "Ah, so! Indeed I do. You would like an Azumanishiki—the rare fish."

The little girl was pleased. "We saw one in the Lakeport 'quarium."

At that moment Nan noticed her father give Mrs. Bobbsey a big wink. An exciting thought came to Nan. Could it be possible?

"Daddy!" she burst out. "Are we all going to Japan?"

The twins waited breathlessly for Mr. Bobbsey's reply. He smiled at his wife and said to her, "Mary, you tell them."

"Your father and I have been talking about it," Mrs. Bobbsey admitted. "We think it would be nice if all of us could go."

"Nice!" Nan cried. "It would be wonderful!"

"Super!" Bert added joyfully.

"Oh, Daddy! Mommy! How 'citing!" Flossie jumped up and down in delight.

Freddie leaped from his chair and pounded Bert on the back. "We're going to Japan! We're going to Japan!" he cried.

His father grinned. "We'll be leaving soon."

Mr. Naga stood up and bowed low to Mr. and Mrs. Bobbsey. "My wife and I would be honored if your family would make our home your home during your visit in our country," he said.

"We would be delighted to," replied the twins' mother.

"Very good. And," Mr. Naga went on, "while your husband and I are on our lumber-buying trip, my wife will show you Japan. It would be a great pleasure for her."

"Maybe we can find Mrs. Naga's gold brace-let!" Bert put in eagerly. "We like to try to solve mysteries."

"And we *have,* too," added Freddie proudly.

Seeing Mr. Naga's astonished look, Mrs. Bobbsey told him of the success which the twins had had in Hawaii—VOLCANO LAND—where they went on a great search for a valuable stone and a treasure of jade toys which a sea captain had hidden for his grandchildren.

Mr. Naga was very impressed. "We would be grateful if you children could solve our mystery," he remarked.

The Bobbseys and their guest discussed the trip for a little while. Then Mr. Naga rose to leave. In the hall he picked up a large box which he had placed on a table when he arrived.

"Allow me to present the Bobbsey twins with some costumes from my country," he said, handing the box to Nan.

The children thanked him and, as he went down the walk, Freddie called after him, "We'll see you in Tokyo!"

"May I open the box, Nan?" Flossie pleaded. Her sister smiled and nodded.

Flossie tore off the string and lifted the lid. One by one, she pulled out four kimonos. Two were brightly colored, with delicate flower designs printed on them. With these were wide sashes with large bows to match. The other two kimonos were dark blue with small white prints and narrow sashes.

"The ones with the wide sashes are for us girls," Nan said.

"Oh, isn't this bee-yoo-ti-ful!" Flossie exclaimed, as she slipped on her pale-blue robe with a peach blossom design. "How does the sash go on, Mommy?"

Mrs. Bobbsey examined it. "The Japanese call this sash an *obi*," she explained. She put the pink sash around the little girl's waistline with the bow at the back.

Flossie ran to look at herself in the long mirror on the closet door. "Oh, I love it!" she squealed.

Nan put on her kimono. This had a white background and a design of bright-red flowers. The sash and bow were a matching red. She too went to the mirror and exclaimed in delight.

Meanwhile, Bert and Freddie had been eying the two remaining kimonos. "They look like fancy bathrobes," Bert commented doubtfully.

"Try them on, boys," Mrs. Bobbsey urged. "I'll help you."

A bit reluctantly, Bert and Freddie slipped into the loose robes. Mrs. Bobbsey adjusted the narrow blue sashes. "There now, you look very Japanese!" she told them.

The four twins walked into the living room to show the new costumes to their father. "Better get used to them!" he teased. "You'll have to wear kimonos on the street in Japan!"

Freddie's face grew red. "I don't think I want to go to Japan after all!" he decided.

Mr. Bobbsey rumpled his small son's yellow hair. "I was only teasing," he said with a smile. "I don't believe boys in Japan wear kimonos very often nowadays."

Freddie looked relieved. "All right," he said. "I'll go!"

Flossie tossed her blond curls. "*I* wouldn't mind wearing a kimono in Japan—it makes me feel dressed up."

The twins were so excited at the prospect of their trip that they had trouble going to sleep that night. Freddie dreamed that he wore his kimono to school and all the children laughed at him.

When they came down to breakfast the next morning, Freddie and Flossie ran into the living room to feed their goldfish. The bowl stood on a low table. The fish were swimming round and round, but kept coming to the top of the water as if looking for food.

On the floor, watching them intently, was Snoop, the Bobbseys' black cat. As the small twins went toward their pet, he streaked past them out the door.

"What's the matter with Snoop?" Freddie asked, puzzled. The Bobbseys had two pets besides Snoop: Snap, a large, white, shaggy dog, and Waggo, a black-and-white terrier.

"I guess Snoop wants his breakfast, too," Flossie replied as she dropped some food into the fish bowl.

The small twins then sat down to eat their own breakfast. Bert looked up from his cereal. "How'd you like to go down to the lumberyard this morning, Freddie?" he asked. "Dad said he'd show us some samples of Japanese wood that Mr. Naga left."

When Freddie agreed, Flossie turned to Nan. "Let's go see Jane and Jimmy," she suggested.

"All right," Nan said. "We'll return their fish bowl."

"I'm glad you children will be busy," Mrs. Bobbsey said. "Dinah and I are going to get clothes ready for the trip."

A little later, Nan and Flossie arrived at the Naga home. Jane and Jimmy were delighted to see them.

"Uncle Mino told us he met you last night," Jane said as the children sat down on the front steps.

"Did he tell you we were going to Japan?" Flossie asked.

Jane nodded excitedly. "Yes. Jimmy and I are going to visit there when we're older."

"I wish you could go with us this time," Nan remarked.

"We're going to find your aunt's lost bracelet!" Flossie announced. "We like to solve mysteries!"

"There's another mystery in our family besides the bracelet," Jane said. "Maybe you twins can solve that one, too!"

"Really? What is the mystery?" Nan asked eagerly.

"Our Uncle Kozo has disappeared!" Jane replied.

"Oh!" exclaimed Flossie. "Is he the other brother your Uncle Mino told us was gone?"

"Yes."

The little Japanese girl explained that ten years earlier, her father and Kozo, his youngest brother, had started for America by ship. "Uncle Kozo wanted to start a goldfish-breeding business here," she added.

"When our father and Uncle Kozo were crossing the Pacific Ocean, the ship stopped at a little island," Jimmy spoke up.

Jane went on, "It stopped there to pick up a man who had to get to a hospital. After the ship had sailed again, our father could not find his brother!"

"You mean Kozo stayed on the island?" Nan asked in surprise.

"He must have been very brave!" Flossie exclaimed.

Jane explained that her father had made inquiries and done everything he could, but had not been able to find any trace of his brother. "We don't know what happened to our uncle!" She sighed. "But our father still hopes to find him."

"We'll find him for you!" Flossie assured her earnestly.

"Oh, if you only could!" Jane exclaimed.

Later, as Flossie skipped along beside Nan on their way home, she said, "I hope we can find Uncle Kozo, don't you, Nan?"

"Yes, I do," Nan agreed. Then she added, "We'll be busy with two mysteries to solve!"

As the girls turned up the front walk, they were startled by the sound of frantic barking coming from the house.

"That's Waggo!" Flossie cried, running toward the front door. "Something's the matter!"

Nan and Flossie dashed into the house. The loud barking came from the living room. They ran in.

"Snoop!" Nan screamed. "Get away from those fish!"

CHAPTER III

FUN WITH CHOPSTICKS

WHEN Flossie saw Snoop, she too screamed. The cat was on the table beside the goldfish bowl. He was dipping one black paw into the water. Waggo was running around the room, still barking furiously.

"Snoop! You're a bad kitty!" Flossie scolded.

The cat gave a startled look at the girls, leaped from the table, and bounded for the kitchen.

Nan bent down and patted Waggo. "Good dog to warn us," she said.

At that moment Dinah rushed downstairs and into the room. "What's going on?" she panted.

"It's all right, Dinah," Nan assured the cook, and told her what had happened.

Dinah chuckled. "Snoop's mighty fond of fish," she said. "We'll have to keep an eye on him!"

23

Bert and Freddie came home at lunchtime. While they ate, Nan and Flossie told their mother and brothers about the second mystery in the Naga family.

"That's some story!" Bert remarked. "I wonder what did happen to their Uncle Kozo!"

"Maybe we can get off at that island and look for him," Freddie suggested, taking another cooky.

Mrs. Bobbsey laughed. "I'm afraid stopping there would be a little difficult in a jet plane," she said. "You'll have to do your sleuthing after you get to Japan!"

Nan sighed. "I wish I knew more about Japan," she said. "We haven't studied the Orient in school yet."

"Why don't you children get the encyclopedia and read about Japan?" Mrs. Bobbsey suggested.

"Let's!" agreed Bert.

In a few minutes the two dark heads and the two blond ones were bent over the big book. The twins discovered that Japan lay in the North Pacific Ocean, close to the continent of Asia. It consisted of a chain of volcanic islands. Tokyo and Kyoto, cities where the Bobbseys were going, were on the island of Honshu.

"What's that?" Freddie asked, pointing to a

picture of a five-story tower. Every story had a roof which curved upward at the corners. Each layer was smaller than the one beneath it.

"That's a pagoda," Bert explained. "There are many of them in Japan."

"It looks like a long way to Japan," Flossie observed, unfolding a large map of the world.

Nan agreed. "Daddy said we'd have to fly to New York, then way across the United States and over the Pacific Ocean."

"Aren't we going to stop at all?" Freddie wanted to know anxiously.

Bert laughed and explained that the only stop the big plane would make was in Alaska, where it would refuel.

Nan had been reading more about Japan, where the customs were so different from those in her own country. "There are many famous gardens," she told the others. "Only the Japanese don't have flowers in them the way we do in ours. The gardens are made to look like natural scenes, with rocks and ponds and little bridges."

When the book had been put back on the shelf, Bert said, "I haven't seen Charlie Mason for a couple of days. I'll ask him to come over tomorrow, and tell him about our trip."

Dark-haired Charlie Mason was Bert's age and his best friend.

"Good idea," Nan agreed. "And I'll invite Nellie Parks."

"I'll ask Teddy Blake," Freddie put in.

"And Susie Larker!" Flossie added. Then she said, "Let's ask Jane and Jimmy Naga to come, too."

"That's fine, Flossie," Nan approved. "I know! We'll have a party! Maybe Dinah will bake a cake for us."

When Dinah was consulted, she gave a broad grin. "Sure I'll bake a cake!" she exclaimed. "You all ought to have a special party before you go halfway 'round the world!"

The next afternoon, the Bobbsey back yard was full of children. The twins' friends were excited to hear about the family's trip to Japan. At first the little Japanese boy and girl were shy, but soon they were laughing and playing with the small twins, and six-year-old Teddy and Susie.

Presently Freddie asked Jimmy and Jane, "Do you know any Japanese games?"

Jane's black eyes snapped merrily. "Jimmy and I can do a tumbling act," she said.

"Swell!" said Bert. "Let's see you do it!"

The Japanese boy and girl ran to the end of the yard. Then they turned a rapid series of cartwheels up the length of the yard, landing on their feet with a smile when they reached the other children.

"That's great!" Freddie said admiringly.

"It sure is!" Charlie agreed.

"Flossie and I can do pretty good somersaults!" Freddie said with a grin.

"So can I!" Teddy and Susie cried in chorus.

Jane smiled. "Good! The six of us will do a tumbling act together!"

Soon the younger boys and girls were turning somersaults as fast as they could.

Meanwhile, Nellie asked teasingly, "Can't you and Charlie do anything Japanese, Bert?"

"Sure!" Bert replied. "We can juggle, can't we, Charlie?"

He got three oranges. After dropping one serveral times, he finally managed to keep them all in motion. Then Bert tossed an orange to Charlie, who returned it with his left hand, while catching a second with his right. The older girls clapped loudly at the whole show.

"You are very good jugglers and tumblers!" Nellie declared approvingly as the "performers" stopped, out of breath.

"We have something else Japanese," Nan told her friends. "Mr. Naga brought us kimonos from his country."

"Oh, let's see them!" Nellie exclaimed.

"We can juggle, can't we, Charlie?" Bert said

Nan and Flossie ran into the house and came out wearing their Japanese costumes. They paraded about amid admiring oh's and ah's from the other girls.

"Bert and Freddie have kimonos, too!" Flossie announced with an impish grin.

Charlie grinned too. "Come on," he urged the Bobbsey boys. "Let's see how you look in 'em."

Bert and Freddie shook their heads, but finally were persuaded to put on their kimonos.

"Oh, Freddie!" Susie Larker cried. "You look pretty!"

Freddie blushed to the roots of his blond hair and dashed into the house. Bert followed.

In a few minutes the boys came out again, this time without the kimonos, and carrying trays of paper napkins, plates, and spoons and forks. Behind them was Mrs. Bobbsey with dishes of ice cream. Last of all came Dinah bearing a huge chocolate cake!

"Yummy!" cried Susie. "My favorite kind."

Nan and Flossie set places around the picnic table under the apple tree, while Bert and Freddie helped serve the ice cream and cake.

When the Bobbseys and their guests were seated, Freddie looked curiously at a package on one of the trays. "What's in the box?" he asked.

His mother's eyes twinkled. "It's a little surprise that Jane and Jimmy brought. Will you
open it, Nan?"

Quickly Nan tore off the wrapping. "Chopsticks!" she exclaimed, lifting up two slender
sticks of polished wood. There was a pair for
each child.

Jimmy Naga spoke up. "They're really from
our Uncle Mino. He gave them to us before he
left."

Jane smiled. "Since the Bobbseys are going to
Japan, we thought they'd like to practice eating
the way Japanese people do," she explained.
"Jimmy and I will teach you how to use the
chopsticks."

Jane and her brother proudly showed the
eager children how to hold the upper stick between the thumb and first finger, and rest the
lower chopstick on the other three fingers.
"See!" Jimmy held up his hand and deftly
waggled the sticks.

"That looks easy!" Freddie declared, and
plunged his chopsticks into his ice cream. He
started to lift a large portion to his mouth. But
the sticks slipped in his chubby fingers.
Splash! A spray of ice cream hit Susie, who was
seated next to him!

"Oh, Freddie! Be careful!" Mrs. Bobbsey exclaimed, as Susie giggled and wiped her blouse with a paper napkin.

"This is the way to do it!" Bert advised his little brother. He worked loose a piece of cake with the sticks and started to raise it. But he had no better luck than Freddie. The chopsticks twisted in his fingers, and the cake flew across the table and landed on Nellie's plate!

Mrs. Bobbsey laughed. "This doesn't seem to be the easiest kind of food one can eat with chopsticks!"

Jane and Jimmy, too, agreed that spoons and forks were better for ice cream and cake.

"We'll try chopsticks again, though," said Flossie.

"You Bobbseys will have fun in Japan!" Charlie said as they ate. "Something exciting always happens to you no matter where you are!"

"We're going to solve two mysteries!" Flossie said, her blue eyes sparkling.

"You are?" Nellie looked amazed. "In Japan?"

The four Bobbseys took turns telling first about the gold bracelet which had been stolen from the Kyoto museum, and then about Uncle Kozo Naga, who had disappeared on his way to the United States.

"It would be wonderful if you could find Jane and Jimmy's uncle!" Nellie cried.

"And super to catch the thief who stole the bracelet!" Charlie added.

Suddenly Bert, who sat facing a row of high shrubbery which bordered the Bobbseys' back yard, saw a movement in the bushes. He watched closely. The bushes moved again.

Quietly he stood up. Then he ran to the shrubbery and pulled aside some branches. There stood Danny Rugg, open-mouthed with surprise!

"What are you doing, Danny?" Bert asked.

Danny sneered, "I was just listening to you twins talking about your crazy mysteries! You'll never solve either of 'em in a million years!"

CHAPTER IV

"FISH" ICE CREAM

"IS that so?" Bert replied hotly to Danny's taunt. "Okay, we'll send you a post card from Japan as soon as we've solved the mysteries!"

"Ha!" Danny jeered. "That's one post card I'll never get!"

"You will so!" said Freddie stoutly.

The bully gave a scornful laugh and ran off. Shortly after the refreshments had been eaten, the twins' friends said good-by and wished the Bobbseys an enjoyable trip.

The next few days were busy ones. Mr. Bobbsey made all the arrangements for the journey, while the children helped Mrs. Bobbsey and Dinah with the packing.

The morning they were to leave, Dinah cooked an especially tasty breakfast. Soon afterward, the Bobbseys were in the car, waving good-by to the cook. Then Sam, who was to drive the family to the airport, started off. Some hours later, in New York, the travelers boarded the huge aircraft which would take them all the way to Tokyo.

Mr. and Mrs. Bobbsey had seats together. Behind them were Nan and Flossie, with the boys opposite them across the narrow aisle. As the jet took off, the twins peered from the windows at the ground which was soon far, far below them.

Then the billowy white clouds closed in. "Ooh! Now we're riding on fluffy cotton!" Flossie exclaimed.

After supper had been served, the pretty Japanese stewardess passed out small pillows to everyone. "Perhaps you'd like to sleep," she suggested when she came to Flossie and Nan. But the children were too excited to sleep.

Presently they became occupied with things they had brought along on the trip—Nan and Bert books, Freddie a puzzle, and Flossie a doll.

After a while, Flossie became tired of pretending her doll was a stewardess. She glanced across the aisle. Freddie was just putting the last piece of a puzzle into place.

An impish look came into Flossie's blue eyes. She pulled the pillow from behind her back and tossed it at Freddie. It hit the puzzle, scattering the pieces on the floor!

"I'll get you, Flossie Bobbsey!" Freddie cried when Flossie giggled. He picked up the pillow and flung it at her.

At that same moment, the stewardess went past them carrying a little tray on which was a cup of tea. *Thump!* The pillow hit the tray, knocking the cup over and spilling the tea!

Freddie looked frightened. "I—I'm sorry," he stammered. "I didn't mean to hit *you!* I was throwing the pillow at my sister!"

"There has been no harm done," the stewardess told him. "But airplanes are not very good places for pillow-throwing games! How would you like me to teach you some Japanese words instead?"

"Oh, yes!" Freddie and Flossie both exclaimed. Nan and Bert looked up from their books, and said they, too, would like to learn.

The young woman nodded. "I'll get another cup of tea for the passenger," she said. "I'll come right back."

In a few minutes the stewardess returned and perched on the arm of Freddie's seat. She smiled at the twins' eager faces.

"What do you think are the two most important words to know in any language?" she asked.

" 'Please'!" said Nan.

" 'Thank you'!" Flossie suggested.

"You're right! In Japanese 'please' is a very easy word. It is *'dozo'*—do-zo. Can you say that?"

"Oh, yes!" Flossie cried. "It rhymes with Kozo. Dozo, Kozo." She giggled.

After each of the four children had repeated the word, the stewardess went on, "Now, for 'Thank you,' we say *'arigato,'* ah-re-gah-tow."

The twins pronounced this word several times. " 'Arigato' is fun to say," Nan remarked.

Their "teacher" looked pleased. "If you want to say 'good morning' to someone," she went on, "you say *'ohio,'* and for 'good-by,' we say *'sayonara.'* "

"Ohio! Sayonara!" chorused the twins.

"Excellent. You are good pupils!" the stewardess praised them. "Now I must get back to my work, so sayonara!"

The twins laughed. "Arigato!" they called.

About nine o'clock the lights in the plane cabin were lowered, and the passengers settled back on their pillows for a night's sleep. The next thing the twins knew, it was morning and they were nearing Tokyo.

When the plane set down at the Tokyo airport, the Bobbsey family got off and walked into the big terminal building, Mr. Mino Naga came hurrying forward to greet them. "Welcome to Japan!" he said with a low bow.

"Ohio!" the twins greeted him.

Their host beamed. "Ohio."

After the Bobbseys' passports had been checked, he escorted them to a large car, and they began the ride into the city.

"Boy!" Bert exclaimed, "this traffic is worse than New York!" Bicycles, trucks, buses, and cars of all sizes wove in and out of the never-ending line of vehicles.

Finally Mr. Naga announced with relief, "Here we are at the Imperial Hotel. I have reservations for you in the new section."

He explained that the original Imperial Hotel, built many years before, had become too small to accommodate all the visitors to Tokyo, and an annex had been added.

"I imagine you would like to see your rooms and rest," he said. "I would be honored if you would meet me for luncheon."

"That would be lovely," Mrs. Bobbsey said.

Flossie followed her father when he went to the desk for their room keys. "Daddy," she whispered, pointing to a calendar on the wall, "the Japanese people have lost a day. It's Monday, and they think it's Tuesday!"

Mr. Bobbsey laughed and explained that when you go halfway around the world you cross what is called the international date line. If you are going West, you lose a day; coming East, you pick up an extra day.

Flossie looked puzzled. "I didn't see any line," she said.

Mr. Bobbsey patted his little daughter's head. "It's only a make-believe line," he said. "We'll get that day back on the way home!"

Later, when the travelers sat with Mr. Naga in the dining room of the hotel annex, the twins were so interested in the other diners that they could hardly eat. At the next table were three young Japanese women dressed in brightly flowered kimonos, and wearing pretty ornaments in their black hair, which was piled high on their heads. All were eating daintily with chopsticks.

"Their hair decorations look like butterflies!" Nan said admiringly.

When the twins had grown more used to their surroundings, Bert's thoughts turned to something else. "Have you found your wife's bracelet, Mr. Naga?" he asked.

The Japanese shook his head. "The police are still working on the case," he told them, "but they have had no success."

"What does the bracelet look like?" Nan questioned.

"It is made of eleven tiny gold fish linked together," Mr. Naga replied. "We Japanese consider odd numbers to be lucky."

"It sounds pretty!" Flossie exclaimed. "Are the gold fish a special kind?"

Mr. Naga nodded. "Yes. As a matter of fact, they are Azumanishiki!"

"The same kind we saw at the aquarium!" Nan cried.

"That's a good clue," Freddie said confidently. "We'll find the bracelet for you."

"And we'll find Uncle Kozo, too!" Flossie added.

Mr. Naga was surprised. "You have heard about my missing brother?"

When Nan explained that Jane had told them of the young man's disappearance, the Japanese looked sad. "It has caused great unhappiness to my family," he said.

After the group had finished lunch, they moved out into a comfortable lounge. The grownups seated themselves.

"May Bert and I go outside and walk around?" Nan asked her mother.

Mrs. Bobbsey smiled approval, and Mr. Naga told them that the Ginza, the principal shopping street of Tokyo, was only a block away.

"Just turn to your right when you reach the street," he directed. "If you get lost, ask anyone for *Teacoco*. He will know you mean the Imperial Hotel."

Nan laughed. "That's easy to remember. Tea and cocoa!"

When the older twins had left, Freddie and Flossie decided to explore the hotel. They left the lounge and looked around.

"Let's go up there," Freddie suggested. He

pointed to a long, winding flight of stairs.

The twins ran up the stairs and soon found themselves in a corridor with windows on both sides.

"We're on an inside bridge!" Flossie exclaimed. "It goes to another building!"

Freddie and Flossie ran across into the old part of the hotel. They hurried along several corridors, and finally came to another lounge.

"What bee-yoo-ti-ful flowers!" Flossie cried. "There must be a million blossoms!" She walked over to a large potted plant and began to count.

"Forty-one, forty-two," she finally said with a sigh, then turned to speak to Freddie. He was no longer in sight!

"Now where did he go?" Flossie asked herself.

From each side of the large room, a stairway ran down to another level. Flossie chose one, and hurried to find her twin. At the bottom of the stairs, a long hall stretched before her. Still there was no sign of Freddie!

"I guess he's lost," Flossie thought. "But he can't stay lost when we're both in the same hotel!"

Cheered by this thought, the little girl wandered along the corridor. Presently she came to a glass door. Looking in, she saw a counter with four high stools in front of it. Behind the counter stood a smiling man in a starched white hat and apron.

"A soda fountain!" Flossie told herself with delight. "I'll go and have some ice cream!"

She walked in and climbed onto a stool. "Ohio!" she said.

The man behind the counter made a low bow. *"Tempura,* little miss?" he asked.

"That must be Japanese for ice cream," Flossie decided. "Dozo," she replied, thinking how nice it was she could speak Japanese.

The man placed a tightly rolled-up towel in front of her and motioned for her to wipe her hands with it. Flossie did so.

Then he set chopsticks and a plate before her. On the plate he put a smoking hot piece of food.

"This is funny-looking ice cream," the little girl thought. But she picked up the chopsticks and with difficulty managed to taste the food. It was fish!

"You like?" the cook asked with a smile.

Flossie nodded. It was really very good. The man, pleased, put another piece on her plate. She was just eating this when Freddie climbed up on the stool next to her.

"Freddie!" she exclaimed. "Where did you go? I was looking all over for you."

"I was looking for you, too." Freddie grinned. "Anyway, I found some stores where they have all kinds of toys."

"I'm eating tempura," Flossie explained. "They think it's ice cream, but it's really fish!"

Freddie looked puzzled. Then he decided, "I'll have some fish ice cream too."

The cook gave him towel, chopsticks, and plate. "Say! This is good!" Freddie exclaimed when he had tasted the first flaky morsel. "And easier to eat with chopsticks than our kind of ice cream is."

He and Flossie had several more servings of tempura. Finally Freddie rummaged in his pockets. He pulled out several silver coins to pay for the snack and laid them on the counter.

The cook picked up the coins and examined them. Then, with a shake of his head, he put down the money. "No good!" he said.

CHAPTER V

TEACOCO

THE silver coins were no good! Freddie and Flossie looked at each other in dismay. What would they do?

"I must have *yen*—Japanese money," the cook explained.

"But we just got here," Flossie replied. "All we have is American money!"

"Ah, so!" The man smiled broadly. Then he bowed. "There is no charge for the tempura. I welcome you to Japan!"

Freddie climbed down from the stool and also made a low bow. "Thank you very much," he said. With that, he bumped his head on the stool!

"Ouch!" yelled Freddie, rubbing his forehead and blushing with embarrassment.

"You bowed with your eyes closed, Freddie," his sister said with a giggle.

The cook smiled down at the two children as they left.

"Arigato!" Flossie called, her blue eyes sparkling.

In the meantime, Bert and Nan had found the Ginza. They strolled along the sidewalk looking at the crowds of hurrying sightseers and shoppers. Most of the people wore Western dress, but once in a while they glimpsed an old man in a gray kimono shuffling through the throng.

"Look!" Nan called Bert's attention to several women trudging past with bright-eyed infants strapped to their backs.

"The babies look like dolls," Nan remarked.

The twins walked on. Suddenly Nan spoke up. "Bert, I've been thinking about Mrs. Naga's gold fish bracelet. Maybe the person who stole it from the museum has already sold it to a jewelry store!"

"That's right," Bert agreed. "Let's keep our eyes open for one. Maybe we can find a clue!"

Presently Nan said, "There's a jewelry shop! And they have a lot of gold things in the window!"

When Bert and Nan entered the shop, they noticed a glass case filled with gold bracelets and pins. The twins walked up to a salesman who was arranging the jewelry. "May I help you?" he asked politely.

"We'd like to know if you have a gold brace-let made of little fish," Bert replied.

"Fish!" The clerk gave Bert a startled look then said, "Excuse me, please."

He turned and hurried into a back room. In another minute an older man came out and walked up to Bert and Nan. He bowed politely.

"I am Okada, the owner of this store. I understand you are interested in a gold bracelet?" he asked.

"A special one," Nan explained. "It's made of eleven Azumanishiki fish linked together."

"May I ask where you have seen such a bracelet?" the shop owner inquired quickly.

"Oh, we haven't seen it!" Nan replied. She explained that the bracelet had been described to them by Mr. Naga. "It belongs to his wife and was stolen from the Kyoto museum."

"We're Bert and Nan Bobbsey from America," Bert explained, "and we're trying to find the bracelet for Mr. Naga."

"Ah, so! Very commendable." Mr. Okada bowed again. "I have heard of this valuable bracelet—all jewelry stores have been notified by the Kyoto police." He paused, then added, "I saw the gold fish bracelet a few days ago—"

"You did!" Nan interrupted him excitedly.

"Yes. A man came in and wanted to sell it to me. My clerk tried to detain the fellow while I telephoned the police, but he ran out of the store before they could get here. The officers were not able to find him."

"What did he look like, Mr. Okada?" Bert asked.

The store owner told the children that the man was taller than most Japanese. "He has very high cheekbones, and a scar over his right eye."

Bert and Nan thanked the proprietor and left the store. "Well, at least we have a description of the man with the bracelet," Bert remarked as they walked up the street.

"Yes," Nan admitted. "But he may not be the real thief. He could have been trying to sell the bracelet for the person who stole it from the museum."

"That's right," Bert conceded. "We'd better start back to the hotel. The others will think we're lost!"

The twins stopped on the street corner and looked around. Nothing seemed familiar. "Do you think we're going in the right direction?" Nan asked.

"I'll find out," Bert replied. He stopped an

elderly Japanese man who was passing by. "Do you speak English?" he asked.

The man shook his head.

"Do you remember what Mr. Naga told us?" Nan suggested to her twin.

Bert's face lighted up. "Oh yes! Teacoffee?" The Japanese shook his head again.

Nan giggled. "You have the wrong drink, Bert!" She turned to the elderly man and said, "Teacoco?"

"Ah!" the man cried happily. He took Bert by the arm and, followed by Nan, led him to the next corner. He pointed down a side street. There was the Imperial Hotel!

Bert and Nan smiled their thanks, and soon walked into the hotel lobby. Here they found Freddie and Flossie excitedly describing their adventure in the tempura restaurant to their parents and Mr. Naga.

The twins' father smiled. "I've changed some money into Japanese yen. So we'll use it from now on."

"We got lost, too!" Nan admitted. Then she and Bert told of what they had learned in the jewelry store.

"You *are* good detectives!" Mr. Naga said. "I have new hope that we will find the bracelet!" He stood up. "I wish to take you to a fine

Japanese restaurant this evening. I will call for you."

"We'll look forward to it," Mrs. Bobbsey said, as they walked with their host to the door.

Later, when the party arrived at the restaurant, the twins were amazed to see racks filled with shoes in the small entrance hall. "Is this a shoe store, too?" Flossie whispered to her mother.

Mr. Naga heard her and smiled. "We Japanese always take off our shoes when entering our homes or temples so that the floors will remain clean. We do the same thing in good dining places, such as this."

Immediately the children stepped out of their shoes. Mr. and Mrs. Bobbsey did likewise. An attendant placed their footgear in the racks.

A smiling, bowing waiter showed the group to a small room. At one end was a narrow stage. In the center stood a low, round table. Flat cushions lay on the floor in front of it.

"Will you please take seats?" Mr. Naga asked, indicating the pillows, and the Bobbseys sat down.

Freddie looked around. "Where are the other people?" he inquired.

Mr. Naga explained that the Japanese prefer a private dining room when they have guests. "I have arranged for some geisha girls to entertain us," he said. "They will sing and dance. Our geishas are very famous for their beauty and talent."

As he spoke, three Japanese girls glided into the room. They were dressed in bright flowered-silk kimonos. Their glossy black hair was piled on top of their heads and decorated with flowers and ornaments. The girls' faces were covered with chalky-white powder.

"How lovely!" Nan remarked. "They're so dainty."

The geishas stepped onto the little stage and began to sing in high, soft voices. Then one of them picked up a musical instrument and started to strum it.

"What is that she's playing?" Bert asked curiously.

"A *samisen*," Mr. Naga replied. The instrument looked something like a guitar, but had only three strings.

"The music is very interesting," Mrs. Bobbsey remarked. "It's certainly different from ours!"

The first course of the dinner was brought in bowls by a girl wearing a dark-blue kimono. It was a clear soup.

"What cute spoons!" Flossie exclaimed, as she picked up a little blue-and-white china ladle.

When they finished the soup, the waitress brought in the next course, then took her place at the round table. In front of her was a large pan over a tiny burner. A platter of thinly sliced meat and bowls of raw vegetables stood nearby.

"This dish is called *sukiyaki*," Mr. Naga explained. "The girl will cook it in that pan."

"At the table?" Freddie asked in surprise. "Mother and Dinah cook in the kitchen!"

"Our sukiyaki is always cooked at the table," Mr. Naga replied, smiling. "In this way, the food is fresh and hot."

The Bobbseys watched as first the meat, then

the vegetables were added. Next, a thin white porcelain bowl was placed before each person. Inside was a raw egg. Over this the girl placed portions of the cooked food.

"Mix it with the egg," Mr. Naga directed, swishing the food around with his chopsticks.

Freddie looked at his mother and made a face. But Nan picked up her own chopsticks and tried the sukiyaki. "This is delicious!" she said.

Soon all the Bobbseys were eating hungrily. They agreed that the delicate beef and crisp vegetables were very tasty.

"I like Japanese cooking!" Freddie announced, as he accepted a second helping.

"Look at the stage, Freddie!" Flossie urged.

Two of the geishas were doing a little dance. As the girls moved with tiny steps in time to the music of the samisen, they fluttered little paper fans in front of their faces.

When the dance was over, the three girls came down from the stage to greet the Bobbseys. Each one wore a card which gave her name.

The geisha who knelt behind Flossie had on a white kimono printed with large red roses. "You're bee-yoo-ti-ful!" the little girl exclaimed.

The geisha bowed her head, almost touching

the floor. "Thank you," she said. "My name is Kashina."

She had noticed Flossie struggling with her chopsticks to eat some rice. Kashina leaned over to assist her. As she did, one of the wooden sticks caught in the geisha's hair arrangement.

"Oh!" Flossie cried and pulled quickly at the chopstick to free it.

The next instant Kashina's glossy black head-dress landed in the middle of the table!

CHAPTER VI

FREDDIE PLAYS SALESMAN

THE beautiful headdress was a wig! For a moment there was surprised silence, then Mr. Naga and the geisha girls laughed heartily. But Flossie's face turned crimson, and her eyes filled with tears of embarrassment.

"Don't worry, little one," Kashina said kindly. "Nowadays many of us geishas wear wigs while entertaining. We like to wear our own hair in the modern short fashion."

Flossie looked up and saw that Kashina's shiny black hair was cut in a very becoming style. "I—I'm awf'ly sorry I spoiled your pretty make-believe hair," Flossie said.

"It is not spoiled," the geisha assured her. "All I have to do is put it on again."

When it was time to leave, the Bobbseys and Mr. Naga went to the entrance hall and put on their shoes. The entertainers followed and stood bowing and smiling as the guests left.

Outside, Flossie turned and waved her hand. "Sayonara!" she called.

The next morning they all left on the early train to Kyoto. For the first hour the Lakeport visitors looked out the windows as the landscape flashed by. Mr. Naga pointed out rice fields and tea bushes.

Then came the sound of a gong being struck.

Mr. Naga held up his hand. "Listen!" he said.

When the sound of the gong had died away, an announcement came over the loudspeaker. "The next station is Atami."

As the train slowed to a stop, Freddie noticed a Japanese boy standing on the station platform. He carried a tray of bright-colored toys. "I wonder what they are!" Freddie thought. "I'd like to buy one!"

Before anyone could stop him, the little boy had run down the aisle and jumped off the train!

"Freddie! Come back here!" Nan called.

"I'll get him, Sis!" Bert offered, and dashed after his small brother.

Bert leaped from the train and found Freddie watching the Japanese boy. From a brightly painted wooden container, the boy spilled out five tiny toy tops. One after another he set them spinning on the tray.

"Aren't they neat?" Freddie exclaimed. "I'm going to get one!" He picked out a top and paid for it with paper yen.

Bert and Freddie had become so interested in the tops they did not hear the conductor call out the train's departure. Bert turned around, just in time to see it leaving the station!

"Wow!" Bert exclaimed. "We're in trouble!"

"What'll we do, Bert?" Freddie asked anxiously.

With a grin of relief, Bert pointed to a nearby door. Under the Japanese lettering on it were the English words:

STATIONMASTER

Bert, followed by Freddie, walked over, knocked on the door, then pushed it open. The boys went in. A man was seated behind a desk.

"What can I do for you, young gentlemen?" he asked in perfect English.

Bert explained how he and Freddie had been left behind. "We were on our way to Kyoto with Mr. Naga to visit at his home," he concluded.

The stationmaster reached for his telephone. "There is another train to Kyoto which stops here in about an hour," he said. "I will notify the stationmaster at Kyoto to meet Mr. Naga and let him know when you will arrive."

"Thank you very much, sir," Bert said.

"Wait out on the platform," the stationmaster directed. "I will see that you get on the right train when it comes in."

Bert and Freddie left the office and walked out onto the platform. Freddie looked gloomy. "What are we going to do here for a whole hour?" he asked. He answered his own question when once more he spotted the boy with the tops.

"I'll help him sell his tops!" Freddie announced.

He ran over to the Japanese boy and by sign language expressed his idea. The boy grinned understandingly and bobbed his head eagerly.

Bert looked on and chuckled as Freddie took the tray and began to spin the tiny tops. Bert bought one. Several people gathered around, attracted by the unusual sight of the small blond-haired boy.

"Come get your tops!" Freddie cried. "Only fifty yen for this super-duper toy!"

Soon Freddie was selling one set of colored tops after another. The Japanese boy stood next to him, making change as fast as he could.

Finally all the tops had been sold. The Japanese lad carefully divided the money and held out half of it to Freddie.

But Freddie shook his head. "I don't want the money," he said. "I did it just for fun!"

When the boy finally realized what Freddie meant, he smiled gratefully and made a low bow.

It was not long before the stationmaster came out to the platform. The next minute a train pulled in and slid to a stop. The stationmaster directed the Bobbsey boys to step aboard. He explained something rapidly in Japanese to the conductor, then the train pulled out.

Before they knew it, Bert and Freddie were

getting off the train in Kyoto. Mr. Bobbsey was there to meet them. "You had us all worried," he said, after greeting his sons. "I guess next time you'd better wait till we all get off, Freddie."

"Oh, yes, I will, Daddy!" Freddie promised. "But we did have fun. I sold spinning tops."

Mr. Bobbsey had to smile when he heard of Freddie's adventure. Reaching the Naga home, they joined the others, and Bert and Freddie were introduced to Mrs. Naga, a slender woman with a sweet smile. She wore a pretty lavender kimono with a design of white leaves.

"We hope you will be comfortable in a Japanese home," Mrs. Naga said. "It is quite different from your Western houses."

The Bobbseys had removed their shoes at the door and had been provided with scuff slippers by a maid. Mrs. Naga showed them to their rooms.

The floor of each room was covered with padded straw matting. In one corner was a small chest with a mirror. There was a low, long table with flat cushions scattered around it. These were the only furnishings.

"Where are the beds?" Freddie asked.

The maid smiled. "When you are ready to sleep, I will put down *futons* for you." She opened a wall cabinet and pointed to a pile of padded quilts. "In Japan we sleep on these, not on beds as you do."

The next morning the Bobbseys agreed that the futons had been most comfortable. After breakfast, Mr. Naga and Mr. Bobbsey left on their trip to inspect Japanese woods.

"We hope to be back in a week, but we'll probably have to be away longer," Mr. Bobbsey said as he kissed his family good-by.

Mrs. Naga now asked her guests, "Would you like to begin your sightseeing here in Kyoto? This city has many interesting spots. It was the capital of Japan for over a thousand years. Then Tokyo became the new capital in 1868."

"A thousand years!" Flossie's eyes grew wide. "That's awful old!"

The Bobbseys declared they were eager to see the ancient city. Mrs. Naga drove them first to the Heian Shrine. Here they admired the graceful buildings with curved-up roofs painted bright red.

"The garden here is very famous," Mrs. Naga said as she led the group along a gravel path.

"It looks the way you read to us, Nan," Flossie commented admiringly. "There aren't any flowers. But how pretty it is, with just grass and bushes and rocks!"

The path curved beside a large pond. "Look at the steppingstones!" Freddie cried. "I'm going to walk over the pond on them!"

"Me, too!" Flossie declared.

A dozen large round stones formed an irregular walk across the pond. Freddie jumped from one stone to another. Flossie followed close behind him.

"I'm catching you, Freddie!" she squealed as she leaped onto a stone just back of the one on which her twin stood.

"No, you're not!" Freddie turned to jump to the next stone. But in his excitement he missed the stone and landed with a splash in the pond!

Fortunately the water was not deep. Bert ran out on the stones and helped Freddie climb back onto one of them.

"Freddie was trying to be a Japanese goldfish!" Flossie giggled. Even though dripping wet, the little boy had to grin.

"I guess this ends our sightseeing for the morning," Mrs. Bobbsey remarked ruefully.

Back at the Naga home, while Freddie was changing his clothes, Nan and Bert talked to Mrs. Naga. She told them that the Kyoto police had found no clue to the bracelet thief as yet.

"Is the museum near here?" Nan asked thoughtfully.

"It is about a five-minute walk down this street," Mrs. Naga replied.

"Let's go there, Bert!" Nan suggested. "Maybe we can find a clue!"

When the twins entered the museum they were greeted by a middle-aged Japanese man. "Good morning," he said pleasantly. "I am the director. You would like to look at our exhibits?"

Bert and Nan introduced themselves and said they were visiting Mrs. Naga. "We're trying to find her bracelet, which was stolen from here," Bert explained.

The man looked serious. "Ah so!" he replied. "I feel disgraced that such a valuable possession disappeared while in my care!"

"May we see the place where the bracelet was?" Nan asked.

With a bow, the man directed them into a nearby room. The twins were amazed to see that the walls were lined with kites. "This very fine collection has been lent to us," the man explained. "Japanese people are very fond of kites."

There were kites of all sizes, some as large as ten feet square, while others measured only a few inches.

"Say! These are keen!" Bert exclaimed.

"And this is where Mrs. Naga's bracelet was on display," the museum director said as he led the twins into another room. It was filled with art objects of all kinds. Along one side was a glass case which contained small carved figures and elaborate jewelry.

A guard walked up. "Hotishi," the director said to him, "our young American friends here are interested in seeing the spot where the Naga bracelet was displayed."

The guard pointed to the glass case. "It was in this corner," he said. "One morning I found the lock broken and the bracelet gone."

"Did anyone who came to the museum act very interested in this bracelet?" Bert asked.

The guard frowned. "Now you mention it, one man did come back several times to see the gold fish bracelet. He told me he was an artist."

"What did this man look like?" Nan asked excitedly.

The guard squinted his eyes as if trying to remember. Then he said, "The man was tall. He had high cheekbones and a scar over his right eye!"

CHAPTER VII

A STRANGE BOATMAN

"A SCAR over his right eye!" Nan exclaimed. "Bert, he sounds like the man we heard about who tried to sell the bracelet in the Tokyo jewelry store!"

Bert agreed excitedly. "I'll bet he's the thief!"

The museum director and the guard looked amazed. Bert and Nan explained how they had learned the description of the man.

"If we could only find him!" the director said. "From what you tell me, I too believe he is the thief."

The twins promised to let him know if they picked up further clues. Then they walked toward the entrance. Near it was a display of post cards.

"Let's get some," Nan proposed.

"Okay." Bert grinned. "But we can't buy one

for Danny Rugg until we solve the two mysteries!"

The director came over and picked out several cards showing the exhibits. "Here are some fine views of the kites," he remarked. "They were taken several weeks ago, and we received the cards just this morning."

"They *are* good," Bert agreed. "I'd like one."

Hotishi, the guard, also had followed the children. Now he looked at one of the kite post cards. Suddenly he exclaimed, "Here's the man I was talking about!" He held out the card.

Eagerly Nan and Bert studied it. At one side of the picture, standing near the kite display, was a tall man.

"Look at his face!" Nan cried. "You can see he has high cheekbones!"

"Wow!" said Bert. "This is a great clue! Let's show the card to the police right away!"

The museum director told them how to reach Kyoto Police Headquarters, and the twins hurried out. When they reached the police station, they were shown into the chief's office.

He greeted the children, then said, "The museum director telephoned me that you have a clue to the Naga bracelet robbery."

Nan held out the post card. "The museum guard noticed the man in this picture seemed very interested in the Nagas' bracelet when it was on display," she explained.

"And his description matches the one of a man who tried to sell the bracelet in Tokyo!" Bert added.

The police chief looked impressed. "You two are excellent detectives!" he exclaimed. "Let us look through our photographs. Perhaps we have information on this man."

He led the twins into a room where the police records were kept. After poring over several books of pictures, Bert suddenly pointed to one. "This looks like the fellow on the post card."

The police chief compared the pictures. "You have sharp eyes," he remarked. "I agree."

He gave the number of the photograph to an assistant, who opened a filing cabinet. In a moment the man handed a folder to the chief.

"Let me see," the officer said, and he ruffled through the papers.

"The name of the man with the scar is Soju Araki," the chief announced. "He has served time in prison for one jewel robbery, and is suspected of several more which have occurred in different parts of Japan!"

"He *must* be the bracelet thief!" Nan exclaimed.

"Our records say that Soju takes odd jobs before he stages a robbery anywhere," the officer went on. "And his hobby is kite flying!"

"So that's why he went to the museum!" Bert cried.

"Exactly," the police officer replied. "I will have my men immediately conduct a search for Soju in Kyoto, and I will notify police in other Japanese cities to be on the lookout for him."

When Bert and Nan returned home and told of their adventures, Mrs. Naga was very pleased. "You wonderful children!" she cried.

"And we'll help find Uncle Kozo for you, too!" Flossie promised.

Mrs. Naga smiled. "Perhaps you would like to visit Kozo's father. He has two grandchildren living with him. They're twins too!"

"Are they boys or girls?" Freddie asked.

Mrs. Naga replied that there was a boy named Tetsuo, and a girl named Kayoko. "They are eight years old. Their father was my husband's artist brother."

"Oh, let's go see them!" Flossie cried eagerly. "May we go now?"

Mrs. Naga laughed and explained that Grandfather Naga lived in a village several hours' drive from Kyoto. It was called Kameoka. "We'll stay with him for a couple of days."

"Grandfather used to live in a town on Shikoku, which is one of the four large Japanese islands," she continued. "The town was destroyed by an earthquake some years ago, and Grandfather moved to Kameoka to be nearer my husband."

"We would enjoy meeting them very much," Mrs. Bobbsey said.

"Good. We will drive there tomorrow," their hostess decided.

Just before they left Kyoto the following morning, Bert telephoned police headquarters. The chief told him the suspect, Soju Araki, had not yet been found.

That afternoon, when the party reached the Naga house in Kameoka, they were warmly welcomed by Grandfather Naga, his daughter-in-law, and her son and daughter.

Kayoko and Tetsuo both had round faces and black hair cut in bangs. They bowed as they were introduced to the Bobbseys.

"We are happy to meet four American twins!" Kayoko exclaimed.

Bert grinned. "We ought to have a twin parade!"

Later, when they were seated on cushions having the evening meal, Flossie spoke up. "We're going to find your son, Kozo," she assured Grandfather Naga.

The kind-faced, elderly man smiled. "Thank you, little one," he said softly. "I feel sure my son is alive. Would you like to see his picture?"

"Oh, yes!" the Bobbsey twins chorused.

Grandfather Naga nodded to Tetsuo, who jumped up and ran into another room. He returned with a photograph which he handed to Bert. The other Bobbseys gathered round to look at the picture. It showed a short, muscular-looking youth.

"He looks very nice!" Flossie said.

"Jane told us Uncle Kozo wanted to start a goldfish business in America," Nan spoke up.

Grandfather Naga sighed. "Yes. And I am sure he would have been successful. Kozo's greatest interest was in breeding goldfish."

Bert had been listening intently. Now he asked Mr. Naga, "Was there anything different about Kozo's tastes in dress or actions?"

"Yes," Grandfather Naga replied. "As you know, fish and rice are the main items of Japanese diet. Poor Kozo could never eat fish. It made him ill!"

Bert was interested to hear this. It *might* be a good clue, he thought.

The next morning when the six children were walking in the Nagas' garden, Tetsuo asked the Bobbseys, "How would you like to shoot the rapids?"

"Shoot rabbits!" Flossie exclaimed in a shocked tone. "Oh, I couldn't!"

The Japanese children broke into giggles. "He said shoot *rapids!*" Kayoko explained. "There are rapids in the Hozu River near here."

"That's water tumbling real fast over rocks," said Bert. "But how do you shoot them?"

"In a boat," Tetsuo answered.

"Sounds like fun," Bert said.

Tetsuo said they had a friend who owned a boat on the river. He and several other boatmen took parties down the rapids.

"And today we have a school holiday," Kayoko said, her black eyes dancing. "So we can take you on the river trip."

When the children's mothers gave their consent, Mrs. Mino Naga offered to drive them to the river. When they were ready to leave, Kayoko put six small boxes into the car.

"These are called *bento*," she explained. "They contain our lunches."

"Oh goody! A rapids picnic!" Flossie cried.

Several boatmen were waiting when the children walked down to the river a short while later. Freddie looked at the men in surprise. "Do they all have mumps?" he asked. Each man had a white towel over his head and tied under his chin.

"Oh no," Tetsuo replied. "It is the custom for river boatmen to wear such head coverings."

Mrs. Naga spoke to the man she knew and arranged for the trip. The six children stepped into the crudely made, open boat. It had a flat bottom and five boards across it for seats. One man took a position in the front, while two others jumped into the back. All held long poles.

"Where are the oars?" Freddie asked.

"No oars." Tetsuo grinned. "The men pole the boat."

Flossie leaned over and whispered to Nan, "That man in the back looks like Uncle Kozo!"

Kayoko overheard her. "He does!" she agreed, and spoke in Japanese to the Nagas' boatman friend.

The Japanese girl translated his reply for the Bobbseys. "Our friend says the man is new here. He does not know where the man comes from and says he refuses to talk about himself."

Suddenly Flossie turned around and called to the strange boatman, "What is your name?"

But he merely shook his head. Then he stuck his pole against the bank and pushed the boat out into the water.

At this point the Hozu River was wide and smooth. The banks were low, and green fields stretched away on both sides. The boat sped along over the calm water.

"I don't see any rapids!" Freddie remarked, disappointed. "Everything's real quiet."

"They are farther down the river," Tetsuo assured him.

Kayoko now told the Bobbseys, "The boatmen have brought their lunches too. We will eat before we get to the rapids. After that it will not be possible to stop!"

In a few minutes the boatmen headed the craft toward the shore. Near the water was a large grassy area.

"This is a good place for our picnic," Tetsuo said.

A sudden idea had come to Nan. "I know how we can tell if the strange man is Kozo!" she spoke up.

"How?" Flossie asked excitedly.

CHAPTER VIII

"MOSHI, MOSHI, ANNO NE"

"WE'LL see if that boatman has fish in his lunch box!" Nan proposed.

The three men ran the craft up on the shore. After helping the children out, Nan led the way to a spot some distance back from the river.

"Now we can't tell what that man's eating," Flossie said in disappointment.

"Bert, you and I can go over to the boatmen," Tetsuo suggested. "I'll say you are interested in seeing their food."

The two boys strolled over to the men, who had opened their lunches. Tetsuo explained to his friend that the American boy wondered what kind of food they ate.

Obligingly, the three river men held up their small boxes. They contained several oval cakes of rice covered with bits of fish and egg. There were also pickles.

74

The mysterious boatman picked up his chopsticks. He selected a piece of fish from one of the rice cakes, and popped it into his mouth. He smiled in enjoyment as he ate.

Tetsuo and Bert said, "Arigato," and walked back to the group. "Well, *he* surely isn't Uncle Kozo," Bert reported.

Flossie was not discouraged. "We'll just have to keep on looking!" she said firmly.

As soon as the picnic lunches had been eaten, everyone climbed back into the boat, with Freddie and Flossie in front, Bert and Nan behind them, and the Nagas back of the Bobbseys. The men shoved off.

"I hope the rapids are *real* fast!" Freddie declared.

Soon the water became covered with little ripples. The low shoreline grew more hilly. Farther on, the Bobbseys noticed the river was full of rocks, over which the water churned in white foam.

"Are those the rapids?" Freddie asked excitedly.

"Yes," Tetsuo called out. "Hold on tight!" He and the others grasped the sides of the boat with both hands.

The river had narrowed, and now high mountains rose on both sides. The swift current followed a passage between huge boulders. The boat was surrounded by sharp rocks and foam.

"This is thrilling!" Nan exclaimed.

Bang! The boat paused for a moment on a flat rock, then leaped forward with a great surge. But the boatmen with their long poles skillfully held it away from the boulders.

"Boy, this is terrific!" Bert shouted above the roar of the rushing torrent. "I'm going to get some pictures."

He focused his camera on the swirling water

ahead of the boat. But just as he was about to snap the shutter, Flossie's head appeared in the lens.

"Flossie," he yelled, "can you move over so I can take a picture?"

Flossie slid along her seat until she was at the extreme edge of the boat. The little girl leaned over to watch the rocks beneath the water. Suddenly the boat gave a lurch. Flossie lost her balance and started to pitch over the side!

"Flossie!" Nan screamed. She leaned forward and grabbed her sister's belt just in time. Both girls fell to the bottom of the boat!

"Are you all right?" Kayoko asked anxiously.

Flossie and Nan nodded as they got up and sat down on the board seats again. "Thank you, Nan," Flossie quavered. "I'm glad you didn't let me fall into the rapids!"

"We must all keep holding onto the boat," Tetsuo warned. "One cannot tell when it will twist in this rough water."

But the remainder of the trip through the turbulent rapids was made without accident. When the boat finally came to the mouth of the river and slid into a smooth lake, Mrs. Bobbsey and Mrs. Naga were standing on the shore.

"They've come to drive us home," Kayoko explained.

"But how will the boat get home?" Flossie asked.

"Yes," said Freddie. "How can it get back up the river?"

Tetsuo explained that the boatmen would walk along the shore and pull the boat to their starting point. "It is a hard trip," he admitted, "but the men are very strong."

"Were the rapids fast enough for you, Freddie?" Bert asked teasingly.

"That was the best boat ride I ever had!" Freddie replied as they went ashore.

On Monday, Tetsuo and Kayoko invited the Bobbsey twins to go to school with them. "You'll like it," Kayoko assured them.

The Lakeport children noticed that Kayoko wore a dark-blue pleated skirt and overblouse. Tetsuo had on a black suit with gold buttons.

"You look nice," Flossie observed.

"These are our uniforms," Kayoko told her. "In Japan, all children wear them to school."

When they arrived at the building, the Bobbseys were interested to see long racks outside each classroom. "Those are for our shoes," Tetsuo explained. "We take them off when we come to school."

He and Kayoko introduced the Bobbsey twins to their teacher, Miss Suda, who was a pleasant-looking young woman. Two children sat at each desk. Miss Suda suggested that Flossie sit with Tetsuo, and Freddie with Kayoko.

"Bert, you may sit with Michiko and Nan with Yoshi," she directed.

Yoshi, a boy about Tetsuo's age, gave Nan a sullen glance as she took the seat beside him. Michiko, the little girl with whom Bert sat, was friendly.

"Welcome to our school," she said shyly.

"I'm glad you speak English," Bert replied. "You can tell me what's going on!"

Michiko held up a book. The page was covered with Japanese letters. "This is our history book," she explained. "We read differently from you. We start at the right hand side of a page and read down, and from right to left instead of from left to right."

Bert said with a laugh, "Then the front cover of your book would be the back of ours!"

The little girl giggled. At that moment the teacher tapped on her desk. All the children stood up and bowed to her. "Ohio!" they chorused.

Miss Suda said something in Japanese which made all the children smile. Then she spoke in English to the Bobbseys. "I have told my pupils that since we have visitors from America, we

will have our music lesson first. We are learn-
ing to play the mouth organ. We would be
honored if you would join us."

A little girl in the first row took four mouth
organs from the teacher's desk and passed them
to the Bobbseys. The other children opened
their desks and took out their instruments.

At a signal from the teacher, the music began.
After a few minutes Bert and Nan picked up
the tune and began playing. Flossie and Freddie
managed to blow several sour notes and then
stopped.

When the piece ended, Miss Suda smiled at
Bert and Nan. "You are very good," she said.
"Perhaps you will play a duet for us."

The older twins consulted each other and decided to play "Yankee Doodle." When they had
finished the lively tune there was applause.
Then Miss Suda spoke in Japanese to Kayoko.

The little girl hurried from the room. Soon
she was back with a three-stringed instrument.

"That's a samisen," Flossie spoke up proudly.
"We heard one at the Tokyo restaurant!"

"You are right," the teacher agreed. "Kayoko
will play it and accompany Bert and Nan."

The three children found a tune that they all
knew, and soon the room was filled with the
melody of "My Bonnie Lies Over the Ocean."

After much hand-clapping, Michiko stood up. "Perhaps the American children would like to learn our song, *'Moshi, Moshi'!"* she suggested.

"Hai, hai, yes, yes!" the children cried.

"Very well, Michiko," Miss Suda agreed. "You may lead us."

The little Japanese girl stood up before the class and started the song.

> *"Moshi, moshi, anno ne,*
> *Anno ne, anno ne,*
> *Moshi, moshi, anno ne,*
> *Ah so desuka!"*

Kayoko leaned over to speak to Nan. "The words really don't mean anything special," she said. "I think you'd call it a nonsense song."

Nan laughed. "We know a song to the same tune. We sing it when we play a game."

"Please do it for us!" Kayoko urged.

So the four Bobbseys stood up and sang:

> "London Bridge is falling down,
> Falling down, falling down.
> London Bridge is falling down,
> My fair lady!"

"Try it, children," Miss Suda suggested.

The Japanese children giggled and sang the song as best they could.

The Japanese boy sitting next to Nan had not joined in the singing. Now he made a remark in Japanese.

Miss Suda frowned. "Yoshi!" she said. Then she spoke sternly to him in Japanese. The sullen boy got up and left the room.

"He was impolite to you," Michiko whispered to Nan. "That is why Miss Suda has sent him away."

The rest of the morning passed pleasantly. The Bobbseys observed how quickly the Japanese children learned. They seemed to like their school and their teacher.

Finally a gong sounded. "That means it's lunch time," Tetsuo explained. "Miss Suda has excused Kayoko and me, so we can go home now."

The children swarmed out into the hall and began to put on their shoes. The Bobbseys waited until the others had run out of the building. Then Bert, Flossie, and Freddie took their shoes from the rack and put them on.

"Come on, Nan!" Bert called as he started outside.

"I can't!" Nan wailed. "My shoes are gone!"

CHAPTER IX

THE KITE-FLYING CONTEST

BERT ran back to his twin. "Your shoes are gone!" he exclaimed.

"Look!" Nan pointed to the rack. Not one shoe was there!

By this time Tetsuo had returned inside the building. When he heard that Nan's shoes were missing, he looked thoughtful. Then he turned and ran down the hall. Bert and Nan trailed him.

They looked in each classroom and rack they passed, but there was no sign of Nan's shoes. Finally they reached a gymnasium at the end of the hall.

In one corner of the big room a boy was bouncing a ball.

"That's Yoshi," Nan said. "The boy who was sent out of the room."

Tetsuo strode over to the other Japanese lad, and soon the two were talking angrily in their own language.

"Yoshi doesn't like whatever Tetsuo is saying," Bert remarked.

The sullen-faced boy was shaking his head and scowling at Tetsuo. Finally Yoshi shrugged, and walked over to a pile of mats. From beneath the top one he pulled two objects, which he handed to Tetsuo.

"My shoes!" Nan exclaimed, as Tetsuo came up to her. "Thank you," she said, putting them on. "How did you find out where they were?"

Tetsuo hung his head, as if ashamed. "Yoshi took your shoes. I made him tell me where he hid them. I am very sorry that a Japanese boy would behave with such impoliteness!"

"That's all right, Tetsuo," Nan remarked kindly, and thought, "I guess there are mean boys like Danny Rugg in every country!"

The twins were having such a good time that the grownups decided Mrs. Mino Naga and the Bobbseys would stay another night. Late that afternoon when Tetsuo, Bert, and Freddie were playing ball in the garden, Kayoko said to the Bobbsey girls, "How would you like to do some *origami?*"

"What's that?" Nan asked curiously.

"Paper folding," Kayoko replied. "Japanese children like to make all sorts of things by folding the paper into different shapes."

"That sounds like fun!" Flossie exclaimed. "Please show us how you do it."

Kayoko ran over to a wall cabinet and returned with a pile of colored papers. She knelt on the floor, and Nan and Flossie sat down beside her.

"Would you like to make a swan?" the little Japanese girl asked.

"Oh, yes!" Nan and Flossie chorused.

Kayoko picked up a piece of rectangular-shaped bright-blue paper. "First you make a crease here," she explained.

She folded the paper as if it were a kerchief to make a crease, dividing the paper into two triangles. Then she folded the top and bottom corners in. "See, it looks like a kite now," she said. Her fingers flew as she turned and folded the paper several more times to make the body of the bird.

"But where is the swan's tail?" Flossie asked, looking disappointed when Kayoko set the tiny paper bird on the floor.

"Here it is," Kayoko replied. She made a few more mysterious-looking folds, turning the paper outside in.

"It looks so easy when you do it!" Nan exclaimed.

With a smile the Japanese girl put the finishing touches on the paper bird, then placed the finished swan in front of Flossie.

"Oh, what a cute tail!" Flossie cried.

"That's wonderful, Kayoko," Nan praised her. "I wonder if I could make something?"

"Of course." The little girl gave Nan a piece of white paper with tiny silver dots on it. "Would you like to fold a flying crane?"

Nan nodded eagerly. She followed Kayoko's directions carefully and in a few minutes set a figure of a crane with outstretched wings on the matting.

"Now me!" Flossie cried.

"How about making a goldfish?" Kayoko suggested.

"Yes!" Flossie giggled. "I'll make a lion-headed one!"

The goldfish was easier to fold than either the swan or the crane, but when Flossie looked at it she shook her head. "It needs another fin," she said.

She picked up a tiny piece of yellow paper and folded it into the shape of a fin. When it had been pasted onto the body of the fish, she nodded. "I like it now!" She set it on the floor.

At that moment Freddie dashed into the room. "Take this!" he cried, holding out a ball to his twin. "I'm hiding it from Bert and Tetsuo!"

Freddie was so excited that he did not see the paper figures on the floor matting. *Crunch!* Flossie's goldfish was smashed under one foot, the flying crane under the other.

"Oh, Freddie!" Flossie wailed. "You've spoiled my lion head! And the crane!"

Freddie looked down at the floor. "Your lion head!" he repeated, puzzled. "And crane!"

Nan explained about the paper folding game.

"I'm awfully sorry I stepped on them," the little boy apologized. "I'm glad one's left."

"That's all right," Flossie replied. "My fish couldn't swim anyway!"

The next day the Bobbsey twins had to leave. They were sorry to say good-by to the Naga twins and their grandfather. But the visitors were eager to get back to Kyoto and find out if there had been any news of the stolen bracelet.

Grandfather Naga, his daughter-in-law, and the twins all bowed low, as the visitors left the house and drove off.

Back in Kyoto, Flossie remarked, "We had lots of fun with Kayoko and Tetsuo. But we didn't find Uncle Kozo!"

"We already know two important things about him," Nan reminded her sister. "He was interested in goldfish, and he never ate fish!"

Bert turned to Mrs. Naga and asked, "Would there be a list of goldfish breeders?"

"There might be," she replied. "I suggest you ask at the bookstore."

Before doing so, Bert telephoned police headquarters. "I am very sorry. We have not yet found the bracelet thief," the chief told him.

After Mrs. Naga had given Bert directions for reaching the bookstore, Flossie said to her brother, "I want to go with you."

"Okay."

The bookstore proprietor proved to be a pleasant man who spoke English very well. In reply to Bert's question, he brought out a list of fish breeders in Japan.

"Is Uncle Kozo Naga there?" Flossie kept asking impatiently while the man scanned the long list of names printed in Japanese.

Finally he shook his head. "Kozo Naga's name isn't here," he told the twins. Then he added, "The greatest center for goldfish production is at Koriyama near Nara. Perhaps you could find the man you are looking for there."

Bert and Flossie thanked the store owner and turned toward the entrance. Flossie noticed a

"Look, Bert," Flossie said. "Here's a kite."

poster on the wall near the front door. "Look, Bert!" she said. "Here's a kite."

Bert examined the poster closely. It showed a huge kite being pulled by six men. The text was printed in English as well as Japanese. It announced a kite-flying contest to be held in Kyoto that afternoon, and another one the next day in Nara.

As soon as Bert reached the Naga home, he hurried to find his twin. "Do you remember the police record said that Soju Araki's hobby was kite flying?" he asked in excitement.

Nan nodded. Bert told her about the poster he and Flossie had seen in the bookstore. "If Soju is interested in kites, he might be at the contest!"

"Oh, Bert!" Nan cried. "Let's try to find him!"

Mrs. Naga too was very enthusiastic about Bert's idea. She suggested that they all go to the Kyoto kite-flying contest. "I am sure you will enjoy it, even if we don't catch the thief," she added.

That afternoon Mrs. Naga parked her car as near the contest area as she could. Then she and the Bobbseys got out and followed the crowd.

"There will be a parade of the kites first," Mrs. Naga explained. "If we stand here at the roadside we will have a very good view."

Suddenly there was a buzz of voices in the crowd and excited gestures.

"The kite men are coming!" Mrs. Naga smiled.

"Oh, look!" Flossie exclaimed, as the first kite came into view.

It was about twelve by fifteen feet and pictured a huge dragon's head with eyes that glared ferociously. The six men pulling it by a heavy rope wore white trousers and short, loose black coats. Each one had a white towel wound around his head.

"It'll go up in a minute!" Freddie cried as a gust of wind fought to lift the huge kite.

"Here's another one!" Nan said. "It looks like a fish!"

As the second kite drew closer to the Bobbseys, Flossie exclaimed:

"It's the gold fish bracelet kite!"

CHAPTER X

THE SQUEAKY FLOOR

ALL the twins craned their necks and stared. The kite was indeed in the shape of the Azumanishiki fish with its knobby head and feathery tail fins.

"You're right, Flossie!" Bert cried. "That's the Lion-headed Veiltail—the one in the design of Mrs. Naga's bracelet!"

At Bert's words, one of the men pulling the kite gave him a startled look. The next instant he dropped the rope and disappeared into the crowd. Bert dashed after him. In a few minutes the boy returned, out of breath.

"What happened?" Freddie asked eagerly.

"I'll bet that man was Soju!" Bert replied. "But I lost him!"

"What makes you think it was Soju?" Mrs. Bobbsey asked in surprise.

"Because he ran off when he heard me mention the bracelet! He must know something about the robbery. Besides, he was tall, like Soju."

Mrs. Naga spoke up. "I think you're right. Perhaps the other men holding that kite rope know something about him."

"I'll find out!" Bert ran down the street after the Veiltail fish kite. Nan followed.

The parade had stopped for a moment to let traffic go by. The children ran up to the first man on the rope. He was short and very muscular with a head of bushy black hair.

"Who was that man who ran away?" Nan asked him. He shrugged and shook his head.

Bert turned to the other kite pullers. "Do any of you speak English?" he asked.

Most of them just stared at the boy, but one man spoke up. "A little," he said proudly.

Bert repeated Nan's question about the missing man. The rope puller said haltingly, "He make this kite. Do not know his name."

This was all the twins could find out. They returned to the others and watched the procession of kites for a while. Freddie and Flossie were particularly interested in the kites with pictures of animals on them.

"I see a bunny!" Flossie squealed.

"And there's a dog!" Freddie pointed out.

Finally, when the last of the parade had passed, Mrs. Bobbsey suggested leaving. "I know Bert and Nan are eager to report to the police that they think they saw Soju."

Bert looked at his mother in amazement. "How did you guess?"

Mrs. Bobbsey laughed. "Well, after living with four young detectives, I understand them pretty well!"

Bert and Nan stopped at police headquarters while the rest drove on to the Naga house. Bert told the police chief about the suspicious-acting kite flyer. The officer said gratefully, "Thank you very much for the tip. Now that it is possible Soju is still in Kyoto, my men can search more thoroughly here."

The twins were so excited at the thought they had spotted the thief Soju, that they could talk of nothing else until they dropped off to sleep that night on their futons.

After breakfast the next morning, Mrs. Naga smiled at her visitors. "Would you like to see another of Kyoto's famous buildings?" she asked.

"Oh, yes!" the twins said eagerly.

Mrs. Naga told the Bobbseys she would take them to see Nijo Castle.

"The castle belonged to the Tokugawa *shoguns* until power was restored to the Emperor in the middle of the nineteenth century."

"What's a show gun?" Flossie asked.

Freddie grinned. "It must be a Japanese cowboy!"

Mrs. Naga laughed. "Shoguns were the military governors who ruled Japan long ago. Some of them were cruel and made many enemies."

Then she added mysteriously, "There's something in the castle which will amuse you."

"I wonder what it is." Flossie's blue eyes danced. She loved secrets.

"You'll see!" Mrs. Naga chuckled.

Nijo Castle was a large, rambling one-story building with a fancy roof. There were enclosed porches around the rooms, reached from a small entrance hall. Mrs. Naga reminded the Bobbseys to remove their shoes before entering. "We do so to protect the beautiful wood floors of the castle," she explained.

"This is lovely!" Nan remarked as they walked along the porch and looked into the rooms with their elaborately decorated walls and teakwood furniture.

Flossie suddenly gave a little scream. She pointed. "The show guns are still here!"

Mrs. Bobbsey smiled. "Look again, dear.

Those people are just dummy figures."

"They sure look real!" Freddie declared, staring at a man wearing a handsome kimono and high headdress.

"He's one of the guests," Mrs. Naga said.

In one room were more dummy figures, this time women dressed in shimmering kimonos. They were arranged as if deep in conversation.

"They're the shogun's wife and friends," said Mrs. Naga. "And next we'll see the shogun himself."

He was seated in another room on a golden throne. In front of him knelt dummies of citizens. "They've come to ask him for favors," Mrs. Naga explained.

Bert had walked on ahead of the group. Suddenly he stopped. Close to the rope strung across the entrance to the last room stood a tall Japanese man.

"He looks like Soju!" Bert thought in excitement, noting the man's features.

Bert pretended to study a painted scroll hanging on a wall near him. Out of the corner of his eye, he watched the man.

Presently the Japanese turned the corner of the wide porch. Quick as a flash, Bert followed. The boy reached the corner and saw the tall man walking along a corridor.

Bert started after him. But as he stepped on the polished wood of the corridor floor, he heard a *tweet, tweet*. The floor was creaking!

The tall man turned around. When he saw Bert, he dashed down the corridor and around a corner. Bert raced after him, but by the time he reached the end of the hallway the man was out of sight!

Disappointed, Bert turned back. He met Mrs. Naga and the other Bobbseys coming toward him.

"Why were you running, Bert?" Freddie asked.

Bert explained about chasing the man he believed was Soju. "Then I stepped on that squeaky floor and scared him off."

"Oh!" Mrs. Naga exclaimed. "This is the nightingale floor! That was the squeaking you heard."

"Is the floor made of birds?" Flossie asked, bewildered.

"No." Their hostess laughed. "It's called that because the squeaking of the floor sounds like nightingales chirping."

Freddie grinned. "That's what you told us was funny in this castle."

Mrs. Naga nodded. Then she explained, "The floor was built to squeak on purpose by one of the shoguns who lived here. He had many enemies," Mrs. Naga went on, "and was afraid one would slip up behind him and harm him. When the floor squeaked, it warned him he was being followed."

Bert gave a rueful grin. "Those nightingales sure helped Soju escape!"

For the next half hour, the twins searched Nijo Castle, but found no sign of the suspect.

On their way home, Mrs. Naga said, "Tomorrow I thought you'd like to see the largest wooden building in the world."

"Is it in Kyoto?" Bert asked.

Mrs. Naga replied that the building was in Nara and contained a giant statue of Buddha.

"Oh, yes, let's go!" Flossie urged. "The goldfish farm is near there."

"And more kite flying!" Bert added.

In the evening they all packed suitcases, since they were to stay overnight in Nara. Next morning, the group set out bright and early by car. Mrs. Naga told them that Nara had been the capital of Japan even before Kyoto. "That was way back in the eighth century," she said. "All the palaces and temples were built of wood. Over the years, a great many of them have burned down."

"What a shame!" said Nan.

When the travelers arrived in Nara, they left their luggage at the hotel. Then Mrs. Naga parked the car and led the group toward a huge building.

"This is Todaiji Temple," she said. "It has been destroyed by fire twice, but rebuilt. This present temple is the world's largest wooden structure."

Freddie looked up at the enormous temple. "My pumper couldn't put out a fire in one corner of this!" he remarked in awe.

The others laughed, as Mrs. Naga led the way into the building, then stopped, amazed. In the center of the vast hall sat cross-legged the most immense statue any of them had ever seen. It was a figure of Buddha, his right hand raised in a gesture of blessing.

Freddie and Flossie stood in front of the statue, their feet apart and heads bent back. "He sure is tre-mendous!" Freddie exclaimed.

"It is the largest figure of Buddha in Japan," Mrs. Naga told them. "His thumb is almost six feet long!"

"Wow!" cried Bert. "I'd hate to have that thumb waggled at me!"

Mrs. Naga led the group through the temple. Suddenly Flossie pointed to a stout wooden pillar. "Look! There's a hole in it!"

"He sure is tre-mendous!" Freddie exclaimed

About a foot from the bottom of the pillar was a large, square hole. Flossie leaned over and looked into it. The opening extended all the way through the pillar.

"Ah, yes." Mrs. Naga smiled. "It is said that anyone crawling through this hole is assured of going to paradise!"

"I think I'll try it," Freddie said. "I've never been there!" Getting down on his knees, he peered at the hole.

"You're too fat!" Flossie teased. "You'd get stuck!"

"Come, children!" Mrs. Bobbsey called. "We're going to see the big bell."

Flossie ran to catch up with the others. They left the temple and walked a short distance toward a massive bell. It was so large that a souvenir shop had been set up underneath!

"I wish we could hear it ring!" Nan said.

An attendant stood by the bell. Mrs. Naga called out a few words to him in Japanese. The man pulled a rope attached to a wooden beam which hung near the bell.

Bong! A deep *boom* sounded over the temple grounds.

"Ooh! That's wonderful!" Flossie said, turning around. "Freddie— Why, he's not here!"

Flossie, Bert, and Nan looked all around, but

Freddie was not to be seen. All at once Flossie started to giggle. "I think I know where he is!" she said, and dashed back toward the temple.

The older twins ran after her. She made straight for the pillar with the hole in it.

"There's Freddie!" Flossie cried.

All that could be seen of him were his chubby legs, waving frantically from the opening.

"Freddie, come out of there!" Nan called.

"I—I can't! I'm stuck!" Freddie wailed.

CHAPTER XI

A WARNING NOTE

"STUCK!" Flossie exclaimed. She grabbed her twin's legs and pulled as hard as she could. Freddie did not budge.

"I'll get help!" Nan said and ran off.

Meanwhile, Bert tried to work Freddie free, but with no success. By this time Flossie's eyes were full of tears. "We'll get him out," Bert comforted her.

In a few minutes, Nan returned with a temple guide who could speak a little English. "Do not worry," he said.

The Japanese walked up to the hole and took hold of Freddie's legs. He leaned over and asked, "Can you hear me?"

A tearful "yes" came from the pillar.

"When I say 'go,' blow out all your breath and make yourself as limp as possible," the guide directed.

The legs kicked in acknowledgment.

"Go!" the guide shouted and pulled hard. Slowly Freddie emerged from the hole. In another minute he stood up.

"Are you all right?" Nan asked anxiously.

"I—I guess so," Freddie replied. His knees and elbows were red and his shirt was dirty, but he was not hurt.

The four children thanked the guide and walked out of the temple.

"You'll never get to paradise now, Freddie!" Bert teased his small brother. Freddie grinned sheepishly.

"Now we can go to the field where the kite fliers are," Mrs. Naga proposed when they were all together again.

When the party arrived, the open area was filled with men and boys and their kites. The visitors recognized many of the kites which they had seen the day before in Kyoto. Even the Veiltail fish kite was on hand.

"I'm sure those are the same men we saw yesterday," Nan remarked. "But I don't see Soju."

"Let's find out if anyone here knows him," Bert urged.

He and Nan walked among the kite fliers. Whenever they found a man who spoke English, the twins asked about Soju. All denied knowing him.

Finally Mrs. Naga suggested that they go back to the hotel. "We can have lunch there," she said. "Then this afternoon we will go to the Kasuga Shrine. It is famous for its many lanterns."

After luncheon the group started out again. Mrs. Naga left her car at the entrance to a large park.

"Look, Freddie!" said Flossie. "There's a pagoda!" She pointed off in the distance where a graceful, towerlike five-story building could be seen through the trees.

"Its roofs are really turned up at the ends," Freddie observed, recalling the picture.

The children followed Mrs. Naga and Mrs. Bobbsey into the park. It was cool and shady under the giant cryptomeria trees. Deer roamed about freely.

The twins exclaimed in delight, and Mrs. Naga said, "The deer in Nara Park are tame. You may feed them. But you must make them thank you."

"Thank us?" Nan giggled. "How can we do that?"

"I will buy some food and show you," Mrs. Naga replied with a smile.

A man nearby was selling rice cakes. Mrs. Naga bought a handful, then walked up to a deer which stood in the path. She held out the cake and said something in Japanese. The deer nodded its head three times!

"How darling!" Flossie exclaimed. "May I try it?"

Mrs. Naga gave rice cakes to each twin. "Just move the cake up and down in front of their noses," she advised. "Then they will thank you."

The children did this and soon were surrounded by the tame deer. When all the rice cakes were gone, Mrs. Naga led the way up a broad path to the Kasuga Shrine.

"Oh, how bee-yoo-ti-ful!" Flossie exclaimed when she caught sight of it.

The shrine was painted a bright vermilion. From the eaves hung many bronze lanterns. In front of the building and throughout the park were more lanterns. Most of the park lanterns were made of stone and stood on stone pedestals.

"Boy!" Bert exclaimed. "How many lanterns *are* there here?"

"There are supposed to be three thousand," the Japanese woman replied, laughing. "However, I have never counted them!"

Nan lingered on the steps of the shrine to admire a particularly handsome bronze lantern, while the rest of her group strolled ahead into the building. Suddenly Nan noticed a short, dark, muscular-looking man approach one of the stone lanterns on the path below.

"I'm sure I've seen him before!" Nan thought.

She watched the short man curiously. He walked in a stealthy way up to the lantern and stuck his hand inside the opening. Then he hurried on down the path and disappeared.

"That's funny," Nan mused, trying to remember where she had seen the man. "I know! He was helping to pull the fish kite in Kyoto. I wonder if he put something in that lantern!"

Nan walked down the path and felt in the opening. A piece of paper lay there!

"A message!" Nan thought excitedly. She took the paper out. It was covered with Japanese writing.

At that moment the others came back down the shady path. Nan held out the letter, and told them what she had seen. "Can you read it, Mrs. Naga?" she asked.

Mrs. Naga took the paper. "Yes," she replied. "It seems to be a warning!"

"What does it say?" Freddie asked.

Mrs. Naga read: "Those American children are still looking for you. Better stay away from kite flying."

"That means us!" Bert exclaimed. "And he's warning Soju to stay away!"

"I'll put the note back," Nan decided. "Then let's see if Soju comes to get it."

"Swell!" Bert agreed. "Maybe we can capture him!"

The group went off a little distance and sat down on a bank of grass shielded from the stone lantern by some bushes.

"We can still see him from here," Bert observed.

But although they waited for some time, Soju did not appear. Finally Mrs. Naga said, "We have been invited to take tea with a friend of mine, Mrs. Yoshida. We can notify the police. That would really be safer."

The others agreed, and soon were stopping at the Nara police headquarters. After Bert and Nan had told their story, the officer in charge promised to send a man to the park immediately.

When they arrived at the home of Mrs. Naga's friend, they found Mrs. Yoshida to be a tiny elderly woman. Her graying hair was combed straight back and fastened in a knot at the back of her head. She wore a dark-gray kimono.

Mrs. Yoshida's black eyes sparkled as she was introduced to the Bobbseys. "I hear you twins are detectives and are trying to find Mrs. Naga's bracelet," she remarked.

"And we're going to find Uncle Kozo, too!" Flossie announced proudly.

"I wish you success," Mrs. Yoshida said. "Tea is being served in the garden. I thought you would like to see a private Japanese garden."

She led her guests to a stone terrace by the side of an irregularly shaped pond. Here, on a low table, were teacups and plates of cakes.

"You know how to drink tea the Japanese way!" Mrs. Yoshida said approvingly when Nan and Flossie picked up their cups with both hands.

After the tea and little cakes had been eaten, Mrs. Yoshida suggested that they walk around the pond. The twins were fascinated as they followed a path which went up and down, across tiny bridges and past clumps of rocks and bushes.

Near one end of the lake was a small enclosure. "This is where we keep our baby swans," Mrs. Yoshida explained. There were a dozen little cygnets swimming around.

The group returned to the terrace. Nearby, on the pond, were two large swans. Bert ran to the car and came back with his camera. "I'd like to get a picture of the swans," he said.

Bert snapped several, then he decided to take a close-up picture of one swan. He crouched at the edge of the water and focused his camera.

Curious, the swan swam up to the boy. Just as Bert snapped the shutter, the bird stuck out its long neck and nipped his arm!

"Ouch!" Bert cried and almost dropped the camera.

"I am so sorry!" their hostess exclaimed. "Hako is not used to having his picture taken. He did not mean to hurt you!"

"It's all right," Bert said ruefully, rubbing his arm. "It was my fault for getting too close."

Next morning after breakfast Flossie asked, "May we go to the goldfish farm today?"

"Yes, little one," Mrs. Naga answered, and the drive to Koriyama was made in half an hour.

When they reached the goldfish hatchery, they were greeted by a smiling man with gold-rimmed eyeglasses. "I am Mr. Kura," he said with a low bow. "May I show you around?"

The children accepted eagerly. Mr. Kura led the group past many large tanks of fish and explained the different varieties.

"Back home we bought a red-and-white one like that fish," Freddie said, pointing to a tank.

"And we saw a has-a-man-a-sheeky in Lakeport," Flossie told him proudly.

"Ah! The Azumanishiki! It came from here!" Mr. Kura told her.

"It did?" said Bert, then added, "Do you know a man named Kozo Naga?"

The Japanese thought a moment, then shook his head. "I do not think so."

Nan explained that they were trying to find the missing brother of their friend Mr. Mino Naga.

"And we have only two clues about him," she went on. "His hobby is raising goldfish, and he doesn't eat fish."

At Nan's last remark Mr. Kura's eyes lighted up. "Wait a minute!" he exclaimed. "Perhaps I *have* met this person!"

CHAPTER XII

A STARTLING GIFT

WHEN Mr. Kura said that perhaps he had met Kozo Naga, the twins waited breathlessly for his next words.

"Some weeks ago," the man went on, "I had a very pleasant visitor who was interested in our work with goldfish."

"Was his name Kozo?" Flossie broke in.

Mr. Kura shook his head. "Of that I am not sure. I do recall I invited this man to have lunch with me and continue our conversation. During our meal I observed that my guest did not touch any of the fish dishes."

"It could have been Kozo Naga!" Bert exclaimed. "Do you remember where this man came from, Mr. Kura?"

The fish breeder shook his head. "No," he confessed.

"But if it *was* Kozo," Nan cried happily, "he is alive and in Japan!"

"You children may be on the right trail," Mr. Kura told her. "There cannot be many men in Japan who do not eat fish, since it is such a common part of our diet."

Mrs. Naga and the Bobbseys thanked the fish breeder for his help. On their way back through Nara, Bert stopped at police headquarters. He learned that an officer had gone promptly to the Kasuga Shrine the afternoon before. But the note in the stone lantern had disappeared by that time.

"Soju must have come right after we left," Bert guessed when he reported to the others.

"Or he could have been hiding somewhere nearby waiting for us to go," Nan suggested.

During the drive back to Kyoto, the twins discussed what to do next toward solving the mysteries.

"We'll have to see all the kite fliers," Freddie announced.

"And all the goldfish places!" his twin added.

"That will keep you very busy!" Mrs. Bobbsey smiled.

When the sightseers reached the Naga home later that afternoon, they were greeted by the maid. "Package come for you this morning,

Mrs. Bobbsey," she said, handing the twins'
mother a gaily decorated oblong box.

"For me?" Mrs. Bobbsey asked, puzzled.

"Maybe it's a s'prise!" Flossie cried, jumping
up and down in excitement. "Open it, Mommy!"

Mrs. Bobbsey untied the cord and lifted the
lid of the box. Inside lay a Japanese fan!

"How bee-yoo-ti-ful!" Flossie exclaimed.
"Who sent it?"

"I can't imagine!" Mrs. Bobbsey took the fan
from the box. "There's no card." She unfolded
the fan. "It is pretty, isn't it?"

Then she looked at the fan more closely.
"Why, someone has written a message on it!"
she exclaimed, and read aloud:

"Tell your children to forget the Azumani-
shiki goldfish! It will only bring trouble to
you all!"

The children looked at one another. Who had
sent the message—the short kite flier, or Soju,
or someone else?

Nan turned to the maid, who had lingered to
see what was in the box. "Who brought this?"
Nan asked her.

"A messenger from the fan shop down the
street," was the reply.

"May I take the fan, Mother?" Bert said.
Then he grabbed his twin's hand. "Let's go!"

he cried. "We'll find out who ordered it."

"Be careful, children!" Mrs. Bobbsey called after the twins as they ran from the house.

They reached the fan shop just as the proprietor was closing for the day. "Come back tomorrow," he said. "Store closed now."

"Please," Nan begged. "We just want to ask you a question."

Grudgingly the man held the door open. "All right," he said. "Come in."

When the children entered the shop they looked around. There were cases filled with all sorts of fans, large and small. Some were of delicately carved ivory. Others were made of silk with designs embroidered on them, while still others were of paper painted in bright colors.

Bert held out his mother's fan. "Did this come from your shop?" he asked the proprietor.

The man took the fan from Bert and examined it. "Yes, it is one of mine," he said, frowning. "But I can't exchange it. Someone has ruined it by writing on it."

"We don't want to exchange it," Bert told him. "We want to know who bought it."

The shop owner thought a moment. "It is difficult to recall," he said. "I sell a great many fans."

"It was probably bought yesterday or today," Nan spoke up eagerly. "Won't you please try to remember? It's very important!"

"Yes," Bert continued. "It was sent to our mother, Mrs. Bobbsey, this morning. We are staying with Mrs. Naga."

The proprietor's expression brightened. "Ah, yes," he said. "Now I remember! A man came here soon after I opened shop this morning and purchased this fan. I do not know his name. He left but brought the fan back later and asked me to have it delivered to Mrs. Naga's home."

"What did he look like?" Nan asked.

"He was taller than most Japanese men," the shop owner said. "He had high cheekbones and a white scar over his right eye."

"Soju!" Bert exclaimed. Then, noticing the proprietor's bewildered expression, he explained, "We're trying to find this man. We think he's a thief!"

"You do?" The man looked frightened. "If he comes in here again, I will notify the police!"

"That would be a good idea," Bert approved.

He and Nan thanked the man for his information and hurried back to the Naga house. When they told the grownups and the younger twins what they had discovered, Mrs. Bobbsey looked disturbed.

"This man sounds dangerous, children," she said. "I think you should give up trying to solve the bracelet mystery."

"Oh, Mother!" Nan wailed. "We can't!"

Mrs. Bobbsey sighed. "Well then, promise me that you'll all be extra careful!"

"We will," the twins assured her.

The next morning was bright and clear. "This is a good day to go out to the Kiyomizu Temple," Mrs. Naga said to the Bobbseys. "It is built on a cliff outside the city. One can get a beautiful view of Kyoto from there."

"We'd love to see it," Nan declared, and her family agreed.

Within an hour they reached the temple grounds. Soon the little party was climbing the long flight of stairs to the brown wooden temple. Mrs. Bobbsey and the twins followed their hostess to the back of the building, where the hillside dropped steeply away. From this point they had a sweeping view of the surrounding countryside below.

The small twins ran on ahead of the others. Presently they came to a level area. Seated on the lawn were a dozen Japanese children. Each one had a sketching pad and was drawing a picture.

When Freddie and Flossie came up to them,

one little boy looked up. "Herro!" he cried with a broad grin.

All the other children stopped work and joined in the greeting. "Herro!" they called.

"I think they mean hello," Flossie whispered to Freddie. She walked up to the little boy. "Ohio. May I see your picture?" she asked with a smile.

The Japanese children gathered around the American twins, holding out their sketches. When they had been admired, the first little boy pointed to Flossie and Freddie, then to his pad of paper and made signs of sketching.

"He wants to draw our picture," Freddie guessed.

"Hai! Hai!" the Japanese boy nodded his head vigorously. "Yes! Yes!"

Flossie giggled and took her place beside Freddie. The little Japanese boy sat down again and began to draw busily. In a few minutes, he held up his sketch.

"Say, that's good!" Freddie exclaimed.

"Please sign it," Flossie asked, and made motion of writing and then pointed to the boy.

The little fellow understood and made three neat Japanese characters under the drawing. The other children all clamored loudly in Japanese. The boy who had made the sketch held out the paper and each one signed his name!

"Arigato!" said Flossie, and all the Japanese children burst into delighted giggles.

By this time Bert and Nan and the two women had joined the group. Mrs. Naga asked a few questions in Japanese.

"These boys and girls belong to an art class in one of the Kyoto schools," she explained to the Bobbseys. "They often come here to sketch."

"I'd like to take their picture," Bert said, pulling his camera from the case.

This made the Japanese children giggle again. They all hurried to join the group and turn smiling faces toward the camera. After

Bert had snapped several pictures, one little girl spoke to Mrs. Naga.

"She would like to draw Bert and Nan," Mrs. Naga said.

The twins sat down on a large rock and posed while the little girl sketched. When she had finished, she handed it to Mrs. Bobbsey.

"Why, this is excellent!" she exclaimed. "And so is the sketch of Freddie and Flossie! I am very happy to have them!"

Mrs. Naga smiled. "Japanese children love their art classes."

The twins thanked their new friends and waved as they left. A chorus of "Goo-by" came from the school children.

A short time later, as Mrs. Naga, Mrs. Bobbsey, and the twins walked into the house, the telephone rang. The maid answered it.

In a few minutes she came into the room with a puzzled expression on her face. "Someone on telephone wishes to speak to one of Americans," she said. "He will not give his name."

Nan jumped up. "I'll talk to him."

When she placed the receiver to her ear and said hello, a husky voice came over the wire. "If you want to find the fish bracelet, go to Takamatsu!"

CHAPTER XIII

CROSSING THE INLAND SEA

"TAKAMATSU!" Nan repeated. "Who *is* this?" she asked the mysterious caller.

There was a click at the other end of the line. He had hung up!

When Nan returned to the others, they looked at her questioningly. She reported what the unknown caller had said.

"My bracelet in Takamatsu! How strange!" Mrs. Naga exclaimed.

Excitedly Bert asked her, "Where is Takamatsu?"

"It is one of the principal cities on the island of Shikoku."

Nan spoke up, "Why, that's the island where Grandfather Naga used to live, isn't it?"

"Yes. Takamatsu is on the northern shore. I cannot imagine why the bracelet should be there!"

"Let's go to Takamatsu and find out!" Freddie urged.

Bert agreed. "Maybe whoever phoned is right!"

Mrs. Naga looked at Mrs. Bobbsey. "We can go there if you wish."

Mrs. Bobbsey laughed. "As long as the twins are determined to investigate all clues in this mystery, we may as well see more of Japan at the same time."

Mrs. Naga explained that they would go to the city of Kobe by train, and take a boat from there to Takamatsu.

"A boat ride!" Freddie's eyes lighted up. "Oh boy! I haven't been on a boat for a long time!"

"You have so!" Flossie reminded him. "We shot the rapids in a boat!"

"I mean a *big* boat," Freddie told her.

Mrs. Naga excused herself and went to make arrangements for the trip. In a little while, she returned.

"Everything is settled," she announced. "We will go to Kobe tomorrow morning and take the afternoon steamer to Takamatsu. I have made reservations for us to stay at a real Japanese inn there. I think you will like it."

All the twins were excited when they stepped aboard the trim white ship the next afternoon in

Kobe harbor. They leaned against the railing of the upper deck and watched the hustle and bustle on the dock below.

After a loud blast of the ship's whistle, the boarding planks were pulled in. The ship inched away from the dock and out into open water. Mrs. Bobbsey and Mrs. Naga found chairs and settled themselves on deck to enjoy the trip.

The twins started off to explore the steamer. "I'm going up here!" Freddie called, and stopped at the bottom of a narrow flight of stairs. He did not see a man coming down them as he started to run up.

Crash! The little boy collided with the hurrying man and reeled back against the wall.

"I am sorry! Are you hurt?" The man leaned over Freddie anxiously.

"I'm all right," the little boy assured him. "I guess I didn't look where I was going!"

The man, who wore a cap and a dark-blue uniform with many gold buttons on it, laughed. "Neither of us did!" he admitted. "But passengers are not allowed on these stairs. They lead to the bridge." He pointed to a sign over the steps.

Bert spoke up. "We're sorry, sir. We couldn't read the Japanese sign!"

124   *THE GOLDFISH MYSTERY*

The ship's officer looked at the children, who introduced themselves. "Two sets of twins!" he exclaimed. "Your honorable parents are indeed fortunate!"

"We're from America," Flossie spoke up. "We're going to Takamatsu to find the fish bracelet!"

"That is very nice," their new friend replied, somewhat puzzled. "Would you like to come up on the bridge and meet our captain?"

"Oh, yes!" the four children exclaimed in chorus.

The officer, who was second in command, led the children up to the glass-enclosed bridge and introduced them to the captain. He was a short, jolly-looking Japanese man with graying hair.

The two men showed the twins the instruments with which they piloted the ship. Then the captain spread out a map and called their attention to the numerous islands dotting an inland sea.

"The Inland Sea," he explained, "separates Shikoku Island from Honshu and Kyushu Islands. It is a very busy waterway."

When the captain saw how interested the twins were, he said with a twinkle in his eye, "Would you boys like to steer the ship?"

"We sure would!" Bert spoke up.

As Freddie made a grab for the wheel, Bert said, "Don't bump into an island!"

Bert had a turn, then the twins thanked the friendly officers and returned to the lower deck. Flossie and the boys remained outside, but Nan wandered into the lounge.

She noticed a large table spread with magazines in several different languages. Nan picked up an English one and seated herself on the cushioned bench which ran around the wall of

the cabin. In a few minutes she was reading a story.

Crash! There was a heavy bump against the wall behind Nan. The magazine flew from her hands, and she was thrown to the floor!

"We must have hit something!" Nan thought, startled. She sat up and rubbed her head.

Just then the door of the lounge flew open and Bert dashed in. "Are you all right, Nan?" he asked. When his sister nodded, he went on, "A fishing boat ran into us! It struck just where the lounge is!"

"I know!" Nan observed ruefully. "It hit right behind me!"

Loud voices could be heard outside. Nan and Bert ran from the cabin. The ship's officers and the owner of the fishing boat were having a heated discussion. But in a few minutes they parted with friendly waves, and the white steamer went on its way again.

"I was lucky not to have been hurt," Nan thought.

Not long afterward the ship docked at Takamatsu. Mrs. Naga and the Bobbseys picked up their hand luggage and started down the gangplank.

Nan called attention to three Japanese girls on the dock. They wore bright kimonos and were bowing low. "Aren't they darling?" Nan exclaimed.

As Mrs. Naga and her guests stepped off the gangplank, the Japanese girls hurried over to greet them.

"Are they friends of yours?" Mrs. Bobbsey asked Mrs. Naga.

The Japanese woman smiled. "They are the maids from the Japanese inn where we are going to stay. They have come to welcome us. It is a custom."

"What a lovely one!" Mrs. Bobbsey remarked.

At the end of the dock one of the maids gestured to the driver of a large car. "For you," she said with another bow. While Mrs. Naga and the Bobbseys climbed in, the three Japanese girls entered a taxi and drove off.

"They will be at the inn to welcome us again!" Mrs. Naga explained as their driver started down the street.

She was right. When the automobile pulled up in front of the quaint, homelike hotel, the three maids were there. The group alighted and went inside. Quickly they slipped off their shoes and put on soft slippers provided by houseboys.

"You may walk about the inn in the slippers," Mrs. Naga explained, "but before you enter your room, you must take them off. This means that you are inside."

The visitors followed boys who carried the luggage along the polished floor of a long corridor. At the end they stopped and indicated three sliding wooden doors.

"We have three rooms," Mrs. Naga said to Mrs. Bobbsey. "One for the boys, one for Nan and Flossie, and one for us. They all connect."

Then she continued, "It is the custom when staying in a Japanese inn to wear a *yukata,* which you will find in your room. We even walk about the town dressed in these."

A little later the children came into the room which Mrs. Naga and Mrs. Bobbsey shared. Everyone had changed into a yukata, a crisp cotton kimono of blue-and-white checks. The name of the inn was embroidered across the back.

"This is fun!" Nan said, parading about to show off her yukata.

Bert and Freddie looked a little embarrassed. Flossie giggled. "Daddy was right. He said you'd have to wear a kimono in Japan, Freddie!"

"I guess it's okay here." Bert grinned. "But I'm sure glad Danny Rugg can't see us!"

"Have you met your maid, Hida, yet?" Mrs. Naga asked Flossie and Nan. When the girls shook their heads she told them, "Hida will look after you while you are at the inn."

The girls went back to their rooms, followed by Freddie and Bert. In a few minutes Hida came in and made a low bow. She was not much taller than Nan, and she, too, had sparkling brown eyes.

"Ask Hida if she has seen Soju," Freddie urged his older sister.

Nan, assuming the Japanese maid did not speak English, tried sign language. She pointed to Bert, then walked around the room on her tiptoes to show a tall man. Next she pushed her rosy cheeks up under her eyes to suggest high cheekbones. Then with her forefinger she made a slashing sign over her right eye.

Hida watched her, spellbound. When Nan raised her eyebrows in a question, the little maid shook her head and burst into giggles.

"Maybe she knows about kite flying," Flossie suggested.

At this, Freddie ran from one end of the room to the other, pretending to hold a string in his hand and to be looking up at the sky. Hida again shook her head. "I'll try it faster," Freddie decided. This time he raced toward the end of the room. When Freddie reached it, he was going too fast to stop.

Cr-unch!

Freddie had crashed into the paper wall. As in most Japanese homes, this was made of checkered panes of white paper fastened on a frame of wood.

"Freddie!" Flossie shrieked. "You're tearing the house down!"

Hida rushed over to the little boy. "You all right?" she asked anxiously. The maid spoke English!

Freddie nodded. "I didn't mean to break the wall," he said sorrowfully.

Hida patted his head. "Never mind. I fix!"

She ran from the room and came back with more white paper. In a few minutes she had deftly patched the torn place.

"Hida! You speak English!" Nan exclaimed.

The maid put her hand to her mouth and tittered. "Only very little bit," she said. "I do not know man with funny face and cut over eye," she added.

Nan laughed. "You understood my sign language, anyhow!"

"What about mine, Hida?" Freddie asked eagerly. "Could you tell I was flying a kite?"

"How could she?" Bert asked. "You looked more like a wrecking machine!"

"You want fly kite, Freddie?" the little maid

asked with interest. "I show you something." She left the room and returned shortly carrying a paper folder. She handed it to Bert. "You read!" she urged. "Maybe kite flying."

Bert looked at the booklet. It was printed in English and gave a list of events to take place during the next week in Takamatsu.

"I don't see anything here about kite flying," Bert said finally. "But," he added excitedly, "there's going to be a meeting of goldfish breeders."

"Oh!" cried Flossie. "Maybe Kozo will come!"

CHAPTER XIV

THE LOPSIDED TRAIN

"LET'S go to the fish meeting!" Freddie said excitedly. "When is it?"

Bert looked at the booklet again. "It's the day after tomorrow," he replied. "Meanwhile, we'll keep our eyes open for anyone who might be Kozo!"

"I just know we're going to find Uncle Kozo here!" Flossie exclaimed happily.

The next day Mrs. Bobbsey told the twins she was going with Mrs. Naga to call on some of her friends. "We thought you'd prefer to do some sightseeing," she went on. "Hida will go with you."

The children dressed in their Western clothes again, and put on their shoes at the front door. "They feel funny," Flossie observed, wiggling her toes. "I like to walk without shoes."

At this moment Hida came out of the inn. She wore a kimono. "You want to go on Yashima Mountain?" she asked.

"That would be thrilling," Nan commented.

In halting English Hida explained that Yashima was a mountain plateau to the east of Takamatsu. From here one could get an excellent view of the coast and the islands of the Inland Sea.

Hida ushered the twins into the same car which had brought them from the dock the day before. After a short ride they pulled up at the foot of a cable railway.

"What a funny-looking train!" Flossie exclaimed as she spotted the cable car. Its floor slanted sharply, and the seats at the top of the car were much higher than those at the other end.

"It's made that way so it will be level as it runs up the mountain," Bert explained, as they boarded the cable car.

"I want to sit at the top!" Freddie announced, and climbed up to the last seat.

"I'll sit at the bottom!" Flossie giggled and took the seat farthest down.

Bert, Nan, and Hida settled themselves in the middle of the car. Then the train started up the steep incline with a jerk. As it ascended, the ground below seemed to drop away. Soon the children caught glimpses through the trees of blue sea.

"Look at all the shops!" Nan exclaimed after they reached the top of the mountain and had walked out on a roadway. Both sides were lined with open-air booths selling souvenirs and food. The twins dashed over to the inviting displays.

"What's this, Hida?" Nan asked as she picked up a tiny flat straw basket. It swung from a horizontal pole held by the figures of two men.

"That is toy palanquin," the maid replied. "I show you real ones. Then we take ride to scenery-admiring place in them." She led the twins toward a row of men who held palanquins large enough to carry a person.

The palanquins were woven of brightly colored straw, and some had little curtains hanging from the roof. The basket-like seats were suspended from a pole which two men carried on their shoulders.

"Oh, I must have a toy one to take home!" Nan exclaimed. "Are we really going to ride in a palanquin?"

Hida nodded happily.

"I'm going to buy this cute little doll," Flossie announced, holding up a tiny kimonoed figure. "She looks like Hida!"

Bert decided to get a penknife with a view of the Inland Sea on the case.

Freddie chose a dried and polished crab. Hida told him that these crabs are caught along the Yashima coast. "There is legend that they hold spirits of ancient warriors."

"I'm glad I have a warrior-crab," Freddie declared.

Hida now spoke to the palanquin bearers in Japanese, then said, "The men will carry two of you in a palanquin. I go in third one."

"Aren't we too heavy?" Nan asked doubtfully.

"These men very strong!" Hida assured her.

The bearers wore baggy black trousers tied tightly around their ankles, and short, loose black jackets. Most of them wore black shirts and wide, coolie-type straw hats.

"I'll ride with Flossie, Nan, and you go with Freddie," Bert suggested. "That ought to make our weight even."

Bert and Flossie walked over to the first palanquin. One of its bearers gave them a jolly smile and showed the two children how to fit themselves into the basket.

The second bearer, however, looked sadly off into the distance. He was more neatly dressed than the other men, and wore a clean white shirt.

With a good deal of giggling the children settled themselves in the litters. Flossie squealed when the bearers picked up the pole and started off at a fast trot.

"Ooh! It jiggles!" she cried as they bounced up the roadway which led through a woods.

At that moment the two men carrying Nan and Freddie passed Bert and Flossie. The palanquin with Hida brought up the rear.

After jogging along for about ten minutes, the men halted and set down their burdens. "Rest stop!" called Hida, stepping from her basket.

The twins followed her example and walked over to the side of the road to admire the view. In a short time the men picked up their poles again, put them on their shoulders, and motioned the twins and Hida to resume their places.

Another ten minutes brought the party to the end of the plateau. Here the sides dropped off steeply to the shore far below. The children scrambled out of the palanquins and walked to the edge of the tableland. The Inland Sea lay beneath them, and the islands seemed to be floating in the mist.

"What is that down there?" Nan asked. She pointed to what looked like a series of huge shallow trays in the water just off the shore.

"Those are salt fields," Hida replied. "Water rise up and leave salt. Called e-vap-or-ation. Takamatsu very famous for salt!"

"This is a great place for pictures!" Bert exclaimed, pulling his camera from its case.

He snapped several shots. Then he called to Nan, "If you'll all stand together, I think I can get you with one of the islands in the background."

Obligingly, Hida and Nan and the small twins posed, and Bert snapped the picture. But just as he did, Freddie made a funny face.

"Freddie!" Flossie protested. "You spoiled the picture!"

"I was trying to look like my warrior-crab!" Freddie explained with a grin.

"I'll take another one," Bert said. "And this time, Freddie, no stunts!"

Freddie promised to be good, and Bert stepped back to get the group into focus again. But he was nearer the plateau edge than he had thought. Suddenly the ground under him gave way and he dropped from sight over the side!

"Bert!" Nan screamed, racing toward the spot where her twin had been.

But the sad-looking bearer got there first. Without a word he began to scramble down the

steep incline. Nan looked over and saw Bert
clinging to a small tree on the mountainside.

"Hang on, Bert!" she called.

Slowly the bearer made his way to the boy.
In the meantime the other bearers saw what had
happened. One of them unwound a rope which
he wore around his waist and quickly dropped
it over.

The bearer below caught the rope and fastened the end to Bert's belt. He gave the signal to pull. In a few minutes Bert's head appeared above the edge of the precipice.

Nan quickly grabbed his wrist and helped him to a firm footing. "Oh, Bert!" she cried, "I was so scared!"

"So was I!" Bert confessed with a grin. "But I still have my camera!" He held it up.

Hida looked pale. "I think we go home now," she said in a shaky voice.

Bert's rescuer was hauled up and walked back to the palanquin. The boy followed him. "I don't know how I can thank you for saving me!" He put out his hand.

The man bowed gravely, but said nothing. The party sat down in the palanquins again and set off for the return trip. When they reached the cable car entrance, the six bearers set down their loads. Then with broad grins five of them rubbed their shoulders and pretended to limp.

"I guess we *were* too heavy," Flossie said seriously.

"They are only making fun!" Hida assured her. "They carry big people all time. You very light!"

The Japanese maid pulled out her purse and paid the bearers. Bert's rescuer murmured,

"Arigato," and hurried off toward the cable car.

The other bearers looked after him and laughed loudly. "Why are they laughing at him?" Bert asked Hida.

The maid spoke to the men in rapid Japanese. They replied with many gestures.

She turned back to the twins with a puzzled expression. "These men say other one not true Japanese. He not eat fish!"

CHAPTER XV

BAMBOO POLE PARADE

"DOESN'T eat fish!" the twins exclaimed in unison.

"He must be Kozo!" Nan cried. "He did look a little like the man in the photograph Grandfather Naga showed us."

"Let's catch him!" Bert ran toward the cable railway with Nan close behind him.

But when they reached the little enclosure, the cable car had gone. The twins hurried back to the others.

They noticed that the bearers were still lounging near their palanquins. Bert said to Hida, "Will you ask them who the other man is and where he lives?"

The little maid entered into a long conversation with the bearers. But when she turned back to the twins she had little to report.

"They say not know name. Man only work sometimes and not friendly. They not know where he live."

"Oh dear!" Flossie sighed. "I'm sure that was Uncle Kozo! And we've lost him!"

"Never mind," Nan consoled her. "If it was Uncle Kozo, we should be able to find him in Takamatsu!"

When the cable car came back up, Hida and the children boarded it for the trip down Yashima Mountain. Soon they were piling out and into the waiting automobile. On the way back to Takamatsu, they talked of ways to find Kozo. They could not decide.

"And what about Soju and the gold fish bracelet?" Nan remarked. "The man on the telephone said we could find it in Takamatsu. I wonder who he was."

"We have only one clue," said Bert. "He speaks English."

"Maybe he was a kite flier," Freddie suggested.

"There aren't any kite fliers here right now," Flossie reminded them.

"No," Bert agreed. "But maybe one of them knew Soju was going to sell the bracelet here."

Freddie had been peering out the automobile window. Now he turned to Hida. "What are all the people in the street waiting for?" he asked.

The curbs were lined with people. They were gazing expectantly up the road.

"I think there will be parade," Hida replied.

"A parade!" Freddie exclaimed. "Let's watch!"

Hida stopped the car, and they all climbed out. "We walk back to inn," the maid told the driver.

"What kind of parade is it?" Nan asked.

Hida consulted a few of the people who were waiting. Then she told the twins that some young men from the northern part of Japan were in town. They were practicing for the *kanto* festival.

"What's a kanto festival?" Flossie asked.

"Kanto is very tall bamboo pole," Hida replied. "Ten times higher than man who carries it. Many lanterns on top. This is to ask for good rice harvest. You see when men get here."

Bert noticed a stand nearby where a vendor was selling paper streamers, birds on sticks, and packages of bright-colored confetti.

"Maybe they throw confetti at the paraders," he thought. "I'll get some." He bought a small bagful and thrust it into his pocket.

"Here they come! Here they come!" Freddie shouted, pointing up the road.

About ten young men came prancing along.
They were dressed alike in white shorts and
loose black overblouses printed in bright colors.
White scarves were wound around their heads.

Every man had one end of a long bamboo
pole balanced either on his forehead, chin, nose,
or shoulder. Built high on each pole were nine
crossbars from which hung nearly fifty paper
lanterns. As the men came along they danced,
kicking out their feet and legs, but keeping the
upper part of their bodies motionless.

"Aren't they wonderful?" Nan cried excitedly.

The first of the young men had come up opposite the Bobbseys. In response to a shouted command, the procession halted. Then each performer in turn made a slow circle, still carefully balancing his pole.

"That's neat!" Bert exclaimed admiringly.

The young Japanese who was first in line gave the twins a broad smile and a wink. The children clapped.

Suddenly Freddie grabbed Flossie's arm. "I see him!" he shouted.

The little boy darted into the street, just as the paraders started to move again. *Crash!* Freddie ran headlong into one of the pole balancers!

The pole toppled into the next performer. In turn, his pole fell, and so on down the street! In a second the pavement was covered with bamboo poles and paper lanterns!

"Wow!" Bert exclaimed. He ran to where Freddie, red-faced, was trying to pick up the lanterns.

Finally order was restored and the parade moved on down the road. As the boys returned to the others, Bert asked, "What were you trying to do, Freddie?"

Freddie looked downcast. "I saw Soju on the

other side of the street," he explained. "I wanted to catch him. He's gone now!"

"At least we know Soju is around," Bert consoled him. "We'll catch him yet!"

When the children reached the inn with Hida, they found that Mrs. Naga and Mrs. Bobbsey had returned from their visit. Mrs. Naga was particularly interested in the story of the strange palanquin bearer.

"He really sounds as if he might be Kozo," she said. "It's too bad you children couldn't get him to talk."

"The goldfish breeders are meeting here tomorrow," Nan told her. "We'd like to go. Perhaps Kozo will be there!"

"I'll take you," Mrs. Naga promised. "My husband would be so happy if we found his missing brother!"

After supper that evening, Mrs. Naga had a suggestion. "Would you all like to go out and see some of the shops?" she asked.

"That would be nice," Mrs. Bobbsey agreed. "We'll put on our street clothes," she added.

"That won't be necessary," Mrs. Naga remarked. "People staying in Japanese inns often walk out on the streets in the yukata. We will also wear *haori* in case it is cool."

At her request, the maids brought the haori—

short coats of lightweight wool. They had wide
sleeves and slipped on easily over the kimonos.

When the Bobbseys started to put on their
shoes at the entrance, Mrs. Naga smiled. "If you
would like to be in complete Japanese dress,"
she said, "you should wear *getas.*"

She pointed to an assortment along the wall
of wooden shoes with large square pegs on the
soles.

"Let's try them!" Nan exclaimed. "I think it
would be fun."

The twins and their mother found getas to fit
and shuffled out to the street. The Bobbseys all
laughed as they walked along trying to keep
their balance on the strange footgear.

"I feel as if I'm walking on stilts!" Flossie
giggled.

The group made their way along the dim
street until they came to a wide highway. Then
they walked a short distance along this to a bril-
liantly lighted arcade.

"A covered street!" Flossie exclaimed in surprise, as they turned into the arcade.

There was a glass roof over the block-long
thoroughfare. Throngs of people strolled
through it, looking into the shops which lined
the street. Bright-colored banners and paper
lanterns hung in front of the stores.

"Ooh!" Flossie exclaimed. "It looks like fairyland!"

She and Freddie stopped to peer into a shop window. "See the pretty umbrellas!" Flossie cried. At the back of the window was a display of paper parasols. "I'm going to buy one!" She and Freddie ran into the shop.

Inside there was an even larger collection. "We have dancing parasols, baby-sitter parasols, and doll parasols. Also, umbrellas," the clerk told the children.

"What's a baby-sitting parasol?" Flossie asked in bewilderment.

The clerk took up the largest parasol. "This," he said with a smile, "is big enough to cover both the mother and the baby on her back. And we have some very nice doll parasols." The clerk placed several tiny ones on the counter.

"Oh, they're 'dorable!" Flossie exclaimed. She picked up two. "I'll take these for Jean and Linda. I'm sure my dollies will want something from Japan!" Jean and Linda were Flossie's favorite dolls.

When Freddie and Flossie came out of the store, they looked around, but did not see the rest of their group.

"They must be in another store," Freddie decided. "We'll look in them all on our way."

Hand in hand, the small twins walked slowly along the arcade, peering in each door.

"There's Mrs. Naga!" Flossie exclaimed. Pulling her twin by the hand, she ran into a silk goods store.

Just then the Japanese woman turned around. She was not Mrs. Naga. Flossie turned quickly to leave. But she still was not used to walking in clogs and her foot slipped. Down she went!

The Japanese woman helped her up. "Are you lost, little girl?" she asked kindly.

Flossie shook her head. "Our mommy is somewhere in this street," she replied. "We're looking for her."

"I see from your yukata that you are staying at the inn," the woman said. "If you do not find your mother, come back here and I'll take you to the inn."

Freddie and Flossie thanked her and left. They continued their walk up the covered street.

"There are an awful lot of stores!" Freddie commented after a few minutes.

Flossie nodded soberly. She stopped to look in a window which displayed a rack of small charms. Suddenly she pointed to one in excitement.

"Freddie!" she cried. "There's the Lion-headed fish!"

CHAPTER XVI

BOBBSEY DETECTIVES

FREDDIE peered at the little gold charm closely. "It does look like the fish with the funny name," he admitted. "But we're searching for a bracelet!"

"I know," Flossie agreed. "But maybe this has something to do with the bracelet," she insisted as they walked on.

Freddie and Flossie had almost reached the end of the street when they saw Bert and Nan standing in front of a sporting goods store.

Nan turned as the small twins ran up to her. "Where have you been?" she asked. "Mother and Mrs. Naga are looking at porcelain dishes. Bert and I have been hunting all over for you!"

"I went to buy parasols for Jean and Linda," Flossie explained, holding up her little package.

"And we have something important to show you," Freddie said. "Come on!"

Bert and Nan followed Flossie and Freddie to the jewelry store. "Look!" Flossie cried, pointing to the rack of gold charms.

Bert whistled in surprise. "An Azumanishiki," he said. "Too bad it's not a bracelet!"

"Bert," Nan said excitedly, "perhaps it's *part* of the bracelet! Remember, the bracelet was made of tiny fish linked together!"

"That's right!" Bert agreed. "The thief could have broken it up and sold the fish separately."

The twins decided to find out what they could from the jewelry store owner. They walked inside. It was a fairly large room, filled with Japanese chests and screens, as well as jewelry.

When the proprietor came toward them, Nan spoke up. "We noticed the gold fish charm in the window. Have you any more like it?"

The man walked to the window and lifted the dainty gold fish from its place on the rack. "This is the only one I have. It is the finest piece of handmade, pure gold jewelry I have ever bought from anyone," he said.

Nan took it from him and examined the charm carefully, her heart beating rapidly. She thought, "It must be part of Mrs. Naga's bracelet!"

"Could you tell us who sold it to you?" Bert questioned.

The proprietor shook his head. "I am afraid not. I did not learn his name. I don't think he lives in Takamatsu."

The shop-owner paused, then added, "I think I can get more of these charms if you are interested. The man from whom I bought this one said he had others. However, they will be expensive!"

Nan longed to ask for a description of the man. But she decided it was best not to arouse the jeweler's curiosity, so she merely said, "We'd like to meet this man."

"He said he would stop in my shop tomorrow afternoon," the jeweler told the twins.

"We'll be here," said Bert.

He and Nan thanked the proprietor and left. They hurried to the porcelain shop and told their mother and Mrs. Naga of the discovery.

"You children *are* good detectives!" Mrs. Naga exclaimed. "Tomorrow may be an important day for the Nagas if you find both Kozo and the bracelet!"

It was long past the twins' regular bedtime when Nan and Flossie went into their room at the inn. Hida had been there and laid out the futons on the floor in the middle of the room. The low table was now placed against one wall.

The girls undressed and slipped under their

top quilts. Nan turned out the bed lamp which Hida had left on the floor.

Flossie giggled. "Isn't it funny to live on the floor, Nan?" she asked. "In Japan we sit on the floor, eat on the floor, and sleep on the floor!"

"Mm," Nan murmured as she fell asleep.

The next morning Mrs. Bobbsey decided to stay at the inn and write post cards. Mrs. Naga and the children walked to the building where the fish-breeders' meeting was to be held. Inside, hundreds of men were milling around in a large reception room.

"How will we ever find Uncle Kozo?" Flossie wailed in despair.

"Let's spread out," Bert suggested. "I'll go down the left side of the room, Nan can take the right side, and Freddie and Flossie, you cover the center with Mrs. Naga."

They separated and set off on the search. Nan walked slowly down the right side of the huge room, looking carefully at each man she passed. This was difficult, since little groups formed and broke up constantly.

"If they'd only stay still!" Nan thought.

Just then her attention was attracted by a short, stockily built man. He was dressed in a well-cut Western-style suit.

"He looks like the sad-faced palanquin

bearer," Nan told herself. "But he's dressed so differently, I can't be sure."

Nan started toward him. "The only way to find out is to ask," she decided.

Just then another member of the group came up to the stocky man and bowed. They talked for a minute, and walked away together.

"Wait!" Nan cried. But her voice did not carry over the loud buzz of conversation. The two men went through an open door and closed it!

Nan stationed herself by the door. "I'll wait until they come out," she thought. "I hope they won't be too long!"

About ten minutes later she noticed a uniformed boy coming toward her. He looked as if he might be an attendant.

Nan asked him, "Do you speak English?" When he nodded, Nan explained that a man to whom she wished to speak had gone into the adjoining room. "Would it be all right if I go in there?"

The attendant threw open the door. "No room," he said. "Corridor leading to side door."

He was right. A hall ran along the side of the building. Halfway down, Nan could see an outside door. The man she thought was Kozo had vanished again!

Nan made her way to the front entrance. Mrs. Naga and the other twins were there.

"We thought *you* were lost this time, Nan!" Bert greeted her. "What happened?"

When Nan told her story, Flossie sighed. "Uncle Kozo is an awful hard man to catch!" she exclaimed.

Bert knew how disappointed his twin was. "Never mind, Nan!" he said cheerfully. "Maybe we'll have better luck catching Soju!"

Later that afternoon Hida announced that several ladies had come to call on Mrs. Naga and Mrs. Bobbsey.

Mrs. Bobbsey turned to the twins. "I must stay here. Perhaps Hida will go with you to the arcade."

The little maid agreed eagerly. "You like shopping in Takamatsu?" she asked the children as they set out.

"We're going to do something even more exciting!" Nan replied with a smile.

Seeing the puzzled expression on Hida's round face, Bert told her the story of the bracelet that had been stolen from the Kyoto museum.

"And you think it is here in Takamatsu!" Hida exclaimed.

"Yes," Flossie spoke up. "And we're going to catch the thief this afternoon!"

Hida stopped and bowed to the twins. "You children detectives!" she said. "I help you all I can!"

As they continued on their way toward the arcade they discussed the mystery, and planned what they would do. "I don't think we should let Soju see us if he does come to the shop," Bert remarked. "He might escape again."

"Shall we hide?" Nan asked.

"I think Freddie and I should stay outside the jewelry store and hide nearby. If you recognize Soju coming in, you can signal us. We'll follow him when he leaves, and drop a trail of confetti. I have the bag in my pocket. You and Flossie call the police and come after us."

"All right," Nan agreed. "We'll do our best."

They turned into the arcade. The shop where they had seen the fish charm was about halfway down the block. As they reached it, Bert spotted a toy shop next door.

"Freddie and I will wait in here," he said. "We can watch out the window for Soju."

The two boys turned into the toy store while Hida, Nan, and Flossie walked into the jewelry store. The proprietor was busy with a customer and did not notice them.

Nan took Flossie's hand. "This is a good place to stand," she said, stepping behind a large fold-

ing screen and pulling her sister after her. Hida
followed. "We can see anyone who comes in."

The girls waited quietly while several cus-
tomers came and went. Finally, Flossie grew
restless. "Do you s'pose Soju isn't coming after
all?" she asked.

"Ssh!" Nan put her finger to her lips.

A few minutes later the door opened and a man walked in. Through the space between the sections of the screen, Nan and Flossie could see that he was unusually tall for a Japanese. As he came nearer they noticed he had high cheek-bones.

"It's Soju!" Flossie whispered excitedly.

Nan again motioned for silence. The new-comer and the proprietor began talking rapidly in Japanese. Nan looked inquiringly at Hida.

"Shop man asks for more fish charms," she whispered. "Says customer wants them."

After a minute she translated again. "Tall man say he go get charms!"

Soju left and the proprietor walked to the other side of the room. Hida and the girls slipped from behind the screen and out the door.

Immediately Bert and Freddie were by their side. "It is Soju, isn't it?" Bert asked triumphantly.

"Yes," Nan replied. "He's going now to get the other charms!"

Soju had almost reached the end of the arcade. "Okay, Freddie," Bert said. "Let's go. You girls get the police!"

CHAPTER XVII

THE CONFETTI TRAIL

BERT and Freddie raced the length of the arcade, trying to keep Soju in sight.

"He turned right!" Freddie panted. The two boys were still some distance from the end of the street.

Finally they reached open air, and saw Soju walking rapidly along the road.

"We'll have to speed up!" Bert exclaimed.

He put his hand into his pocket and pulled out the package of confetti. Bert began to drop pieces of the bright-colored paper onto the road as the brothers ran after Soju.

When the two boys were about half a block behind the tall Japanese, they slowed down. "We don't want him to know he's being followed," Bert cautioned.

At that moment Soju crossed the road and

turned down a narrow lane. After that he made several more turns.

At one time Bert and Freddie thought they had lost him. They paused at a corner and looked both ways. There was no sign of Soju!

"He mustn't get away now!" Freddie cried.

Bert looked around. "There he is!" Through the open space between two houses, they saw Soju still striding ahead, up a narrow street.

"I hope the confetti holds out!" Bert said, as he and Freddie continued their pursuit.

Just then the tall man stopped in front of a small cottage. It was one story high and built of brown wood. There was a bamboo fence with a gate, and a garden at one side.

Soju opened the gate and walked into the garden. Bert and Freddie ran forward and crouched down beside the fence.

"Can you see Soju?" Freddie whispered.

Bert had found a wide slit in the fence and pointed to a small shed near one corner of the house. Soju was just going into it. In a few moments he came out with a spade. He looked around carefully, then began to dig in the ground alongside the house.

In the meantime Nan, Flossie, and Hida had run back through the arcade to the highway where Hida said there would be a policeman.

"We must find an officer quickly!" Nan exclaimed.

The maid pointed up the road. A Japanese policeman was approaching on a bicycle.

"Stop him, Hida!" Flossie begged, jumping up and down in excitement.

When Hida signaled to the officer, he pulled over to the side of the road with an inquiring look. In rapid Japanese Hida explained the situation.

The man looked at Nan and Flossie in surprise. "So you think you are on the trail of a thief?" he asked.

"You speak English!" Nan cried in relief. "Can you come with us now?"

The policeman nodded. With Hida and the girls running along beside him, he pedaled into the arcade.

"This is the shop where we saw Soju!" Nan said as they passed it.

The officer frowned. "Did you say Soju?"

"Yes," Nan replied. "He's Soju Araki. We picked out his picture for the Kyoto police."

"So you are the ones who did that!" the policeman exclaimed. "All the police in Japan have been alerted to watch for Soju. You're sure he is the man you saw this afternoon?"

Nan and Flossie both nodded vigorously. By

this time the group had reached the end of the arcade. "Now we look for the confetti trail," Nan said.

Flossie spotted it. The policeman parked his bicycle. "We will follow it on foot," he said.

The four hurried up the road for several blocks. The confetti trail abruptly ended. "Oh, no!" Nan cried in despair.

But Hida's sharp eyes spotted a few bits of bright color in the middle of the road. "I think the boys cross here," she observed.

The group dashed to the other side of the street. Here they saw more pieces of confetti, and soon the trail led down the narrow side road.

The searchers made their way along the twisting, narrow streets. Several times the trail seemed to vanish. Then one of the group would detect another bit of confetti to set them on the track again.

Suddenly, when they had just turned another corner, Nan, who was in the lead, put up her hand. "There are Bert and Freddie—crouching by that fence!" she whispered.

At that moment Bert looked around. When he saw the girls with the policeman, he motioned them to come forward. They all crept up and joined the two boys.

"Soju is digging up something," Bert whispered to the policeman, pointing out the wide slit in the fence.

At that moment the suspect lifted a small package from the hole which he had dug.

The policeman leaped up, rushed through the gate toward Soju, and called out, "I will take that!" Bert and Freddie followed close behind.

The tall man whirled about. When he saw the trio advancing on him, he turned to run. But Bert and Freddie were too quick for him.

"Let's get him, Freddie!" Bert yelled as he made a flying tackle and grabbed Soju around the waist. Freddie flung himself forward and caught one of the man's ankles. He clung to it tightly.

"Very good, boys!" the policeman said. He stepped up and snapped handcuffs on the struggling prisoner.

Nan picked up the package which Soju had dropped in the confusion. She undid the wrapping. There, on a layer of cotton, lay ten tiny carved gold fish!

"It *is* Mrs. Naga's stolen bracelet!" she cried in triumph.

The policeman nudged his prisoner. "What do you have to say?"

"I took the bracelet," Soju confessed sullenly, "and broke it into eleven parts so it would be easier to sell."

"I found the fish charm in the arcade shop!" Flossie told him proudly.

"We saw you in the shop today," Freddie said to Soju.

The prisoner muttered, "I am disgraced! To be caught by four children!" He glared at them. "I found the warning in the stone lantern my friend put there. But I did not think you could catch me!"

"You will come with me now," the officer said sternly to his prisoner.

At that moment a stocky, dark-haired man opened the gate and came into the garden. The twins looked at him, then at one another in astonishment. This was the man they believed to be Kozo Naga!

Before they could ask him, the man said something in Japanese. The officer replied, indicating the children with a sweep of his hand.

"Ah, so!" the stocky man said in English. "Now I recognize these children. They are the little American twins who were on Yashima yesterday. But, officer, where are you taking my helper?"

"Your helper!" Bert echoed. "Do you live here?"

"Yes."

"What do *you* know about this man?" the policeman asked him suspiciously.

"Very little," the owner of the house replied. "I am a fish breeder. I hired him just yesterday to help me take care of the fish."

"These American children," the policeman explained in English, "have been trying to solve the mystery of a valuable bracelet which disappeared from the Kyoto museum. They trailed this man and discovered him digging up charms from the bracelet in your garden. We believe he is Soju Araki, the notorious jewel thief!"

The fish breeder looked shocked. "Stolen bracelet—in my garden!" he exclaimed. "I assure you I knew nothing of this!"

The officer nodded. "I believe you," he said. "But the chief will wish you to come to headquarters later and testify." Then he turned to the twins. "I now take the prisoner to police station." He went off with the thief.

"We go back to inn?" Hida suggested.

"Please wait a minute!" Nan begged. She looked directly at the fish breeder. "Are you Kozo Naga?" she asked.

CHAPTER XVIII

"SAYONARA!"

THE stocky, dark-haired man stared at Nan. The twins waited tensely for his answer.

Finally he spoke. "Yes, I am Kozo Naga. How did you know?"

"We knew you got lost on the way to America," Freddie said. "And that you liked raising goldfish."

"And Grandfather Naga told us you wouldn't eat fish," Flossie added.

"Grandfather Naga!" Kozo exclaimed. "You mean my father is alive!"

Nan and Bert then told the amazed fish breeder the full story of their search for him.

"You are wonderful children!" he said happily. "I must go to my father at once!"

Bert told Kozo they were staying at the inn with Mrs. Mino Naga. "I must call on her," he

167

said, "and hear all about my family, both in America and in Japan."

Mrs. Naga was overjoyed when the twins walked into the inn with Kozo. "Although I never knew you," she said to him, "I have heard much about you from my husband. Also, Grandfather talks of you constantly. We must let him know right away that you are alive!"

She went with Kozo to the telephone to call the Nagas in Kameoka. When they returned Kozo was beaming with happiness. "We are all going to Kameoka as soon as possible!" he said.

"But please tell us what happened when you disappeared!" Nan urged as they all sat in the garden a little later.

Kozo sighed. "I was young and thoughtless then. After our ship stopped at the Pacific island, I went in search of a fish pond. I thought I might find an unusual kind of goldfish."

"Did you?" Flossie asked excitedly.

Kozo shook his head. "No. By the time I got back to the dock, the ship had left. There was no way to communicate with it."

"What did you do next?" Freddie asked.

"Some kind people took me in, and I stayed on the island for almost a year before another ship touched there. It was going to Japan so I came back here." The man swallowed hard.

Finally he continued, "When I reached my native village again, I found it had been destroyed by an earthquake. No one knew whether my father and brothers had escaped or not!"

"Why didn't you write to your brother in America?" Bert asked curiously.

Kozo looked sad. "I did not know where he had gone. America is very large!"

"How awful for you!" Nan said.

"Yes, it was," he agreed. "Since I was unable to find my father and brothers, I came to Takamatsu and began to raise fish."

"And carry people in palanquins!" Flossie put in.

Kozo smiled at the little girl. "Yes, I did so to earn more money to buy fish!"

At that moment Bert was summoned to the telephone. When he came back, he reported that the call had been from the police chief.

"Mrs. Naga, he wants you to come to headquarters tomorrow to identify the bracelet. And we twins are to go, too."

When they arrived, the chief welcomed them warmly. "You children have done us a great service in catching this jewel thief!" he said. "We would like you to make the identification official."

Soju Araki was brought into the room. He glared at the children.

"Is this the man whose picture you saw in the police files in Kyoto?" the chief asked the twins.

They nodded. The officer showed Mrs. Naga the eleven tiny carved fish. She assured him that they were the pieces of the bracelet which had been stolen from the Kyoto museum.

While the chief was writing his report, Soju asked sullenly, "How did you know I would be in Takamatsu?"

"Someone called us in Kyoto and told us," Nan replied.

"I know who that was!" Soju snarled. "A man who was supposed to be my friend. He knew I had taken the bracelet. When I wouldn't promise him to split the money I got for it, he told you where I had gone!"

After Soju had been led from the room, the chief told Mrs. Naga he was sure the bracelet could be restored perfectly.

As the group left headquarters, Mrs. Naga said happily, "We can fly home this afternoon! A message came this morning at the inn that my husband and Mr. Bobbsey are arriving in Kyoto today!"

"Goody!" Flossie cried. "We have so much to tell them!"

"There's one thing I'm going to do right away!" Bert announced. "Send a post card to Danny Rugg and let him know we've solved both mysteries!"

"And let's send one to Jane and Jimmy and tell them we've found Uncle Kozo!" Flossie said to her twin.

As soon as they returned to the inn, the two women, with Hida's help, packed for the return journey to Kyoto. Meanwhile, the twins stopped in a nearby shop to buy the cards.

"Here's one for Danny!" Freddie laughed, and picked up a picture of a warrior crab.

Bert addressed the card, then wrote:

Dear Danny: This is the card you said you'd never get! We have solved both mysteries. See you soon! The Bobbsey Twins.

Flossie picked out a card showing several kinds of goldfish for Jane and Jimmy Naga. On it she printed the message: *We found Uncle Kozo. He raises fish.*

When it was time to leave the inn, Mrs. Naga and the Bobbseys said good-by to Hida and set off for the airport. Kozo Naga joined them there.

The flight back to Kyoto was short. When the plane set down, Mr. Naga and Mr. Bobbsey were waiting for them.

"Kozo!"

"Mino!"

The two Naga brothers greeted each other joyfully. Then Mino Naga turned to the twins. "I little dreamed when I invited you to Japan, that you would find my long-lost brother!"

"We found the gold fish bracelet, too!" Freddie piped up.

On the drive home the twins took turns relating all their adventures to their father and Mr. Naga. Kozo then reminded everyone, "My father is expecting us all to come to Kameoka for a reunion."

"Fine!" Mino Naga said. "We will go tomorrow."

The Bobbseys and Nagas were warmly welcomed the next day in Kameoka. Grandfather Naga was overjoyed to see Kozo.

"We will have a formal Japanese dinner in honor of our visitors," the elderly man announced.

Later, the happy families all took places on the floor cushions. A small tray was set in front of each person. It contained a bowl of clear soup and another of fish. After this first course, three more trays were set at each place. These contained the main dishes of the meal: rice, meat, vegetables, and tiny cakes.

At the end of the dinner, Grandfather Naga stood up. "We are deeply grateful to our little American friends for the service they have rendered to the Naga family. We wish to give the twins small *presentos!*"

The children watched with eager interest as Kayoko and Tetsuo arose and hurried from the room. When the Japanese twins returned, they gave each of the Bobbsey twins a beautifully wrapped package.

"Open them," the kindly grandfather urged.

Flossie unwrapped hers first. Inside the box was a pendant on a thin gold chain. It was a tiny gold fish with pearl eyes. "It's a telephone fish!" Flossie cried in excitement. "Like one I saw at the fish farm!"

Nan laughed. "I think you mean a telescope fish, Flossie," she said.

"I guess you're right. Open yours, Nan!"

Nan's gift was a Japanese bride doll. The delicate figure was dressed in a kimono of cream-colored silk. Around her elaborate headdress was a broad, jeweled band.

"How lovely!" Nan breathed. "She will be the prize of my doll collection."

Freddie could wait no longer. "May I open my presento now?" he asked eagerly.

"Certainly," Grandfather Naga nodded.

Freddie tore off the paper from a large box. Inside were kites with strange Oriental figures painted on them. There was a dragon breathing fire, a goldfish with double tail fins, and a soldier wearing a fierce expression.

The little boy's eyes shone. "Oh boy!" he exclaimed. "Wait till I fly these in Lakeport!"

"What is in your package, Bert?" Nan asked.

Bert was speechless when he opened his gift. It was a tiny flash camera!

"It's all ready to use!" Tetsuo spoke up. "There's a roll of film in it."

"This is terrific!" Bert said happily. "May I take your pictures now?"

When Grandfather Naga smiled assent, Bert moved to the end of the room and photographed the group.

"I wish we didn't have to leave," Nan said wistfully. "I love Japan and everyone in it!"

"Even Soju?" Bert teased.

When the Bobbseys were ready to start back to Kyoto the next morning, Bert said to Kayoko and Tetsuo, "You must come see us in Lakeport."

"We will!" Tetsuo replied. "Maybe Uncle Kozo will take us with him when he goes to America!"

"But, don't let him get off the boat before you get there," Flossie advised impishly.

As Mr. and Mrs. Mino Naga and the Bobbsey family drove off, Grandfather Naga, Uncle Kozo, the Japanese twins, and their mother cried, "Sayonara! Sayonara!"

"Sayonara!" the Bobbseys called back.

DETACH ALONG DOTTED LINE AND MAIL IN ENVELOPE WITH PAYMENT